DANGEROUSLY DELICIOUS

When Quinn went to the kitchen counter for the donuts, he came back empty-handed. "Sorry," he said, abandoning the script. "There aren't any donuts?"

"Props!" Audrey shouted, fuming. "Where are the donuts?"

We all looked around for Marco, the prop guy, but he was nowhere to be seen.

"Will somebody please go to the prop room and get the donuts?" the director shouted from the control booth.

"I'll go," Kandi said. Minutes later, she returned with the donuts.

"Okay," the director called out. "Let's take it from the top."

This time there was a pastry box on the counter. Quinn brought it back to the table.

"Sure you won't have one?"

He held out the box to Mr. Watkins, but Watkins waved it away.

"You'll be sorry," Quinn said, plucking a sugar-coated donut from the box. But as it turned out, Quinn was the sorry one. He took one mouthful and grimaced.

"I think there's something wrong with this do—"

But before he could utter his last "nut," he doubled over in pain, his fac   of blue . . .

Books by Laura Levine

THIS PEN FOR HIRE

LAST WRITES

KILLER BLONDE

Published by Kensington Publishing Corporation

A Jaine Austen Mystery

Last Writes

Laura Levine

KENSINGTON BOOKS
Kensington Publishing Corp.
http://www.kensingtonbooks.com

KENSINGTON BOOKS are published by

Kensington Publishing Corp.
850 Third Avenue
New York, NY 10022

All Kensington Titles, Imprints, and Distributed Lines are available at special quantity discounts for bulk purchases for sales promotions, premiums, fund-raising, and educational or institutional use. Special book excerpts or customized printings can also be created to fit specific needs. For details, write or phone the office of the Kensington special sales manager: Kensington Publishing Corp., 850 Third Avenue, New York, NY 10022, attn: Special Sales Department, Phone: 1-800-221-2647.

Kensington and the K logo Reg. U.S. Pat. & TM Off.

First Kensington hardcover printing: July 2003
First Kensington mass market printing: June 2004

10 9 8 7 6 5 4 3 2 1

Printed in the United States of America

For D.W.P.

ACKNOWLEDGMENTS

Many thanks to my agent, Evan Marshall, and my editor, John Scognamiglio, for their guidance and support. And thanks also to my cat Mr. Guy, without whose constant demands for food this book would have been finished a whole lot sooner.

Chapter One

I should've known there was trouble ahead when I saw the sign over the studio gate:

MIRACLE STUDIOS
"If It's a Good Picture, It's a Miracle"

Miracle Studios, for those of you lucky enough never to have been there, is a sorry collection of soundstages in the scuzziest section of Hollywood, a part of town where the hookers outnumber the parking meters two to one.

But when I drove onto the Miracle lot that hazy Monday morning, I was a happy camper. I, Jaine Austen, was about to become a bona fide Hollywood Sitcom Writer. After years of toiling at my computer as a freelance writer, churning out brochures and resumes and personals ads, I was about to strike it rich in show biz. No longer would I have to come up with fictional resumes for college grads with room-temperature IQs. Or slogans for my biggest client, Toiletmasters Plumbers (*In a Rush to Flush? Call Toiletmasters*).

I owed my good fortune to my best friend, Kandi

Tobolowski. Six weeks earlier, she'd called me with the news:

"Guess what," she said. "I've kissed the cockroach good-bye!"

The cockroach to whom she was referring was the star insect of a Saturday morning cartoon show, *Beanie & The Cockroach*, a heartwarming saga of a chef named Beanie and his pet cockroach, Fred. Kandi had been a staff writer on *Beanie* for more years than she cared to admit. Like most animation writers, she'd long dreamed of landing a job in the far more prestigious world of live-action television.

And that day had finally arrived. Her agent had taken enough time off from lunch at Spago to line up a job for her on a comedy called *Muffy 'n Me*—a Saturday morning syndicated show about a buxom teenage girl who gets hit on the head with a volleyball and develops magical powers.

As the Miracle bigwigs pitched it to the network, "It's *Bewitched* with tits."

Okay, so it wasn't going to win any Emmys. But it was a big step up from the cockroach, and Kandi was thrilled. So was I, two weeks later, when she told me she'd managed to get me a script assignment on the show.

At first, I was terrified. After all, I wasn't much of a comedy writer. But then *Muffy 'n Me* wasn't much of a comedy. So, after chaining myself to my computer, armed with only my wits and a copy of Henny Youngman's *Giant Book of One-Liners*, I managed to complete my comedic masterpiece, "Cinderella Muffy." It's all about what happens when Muffy magically changes her ratty bathrobe into a glam prom dress, only to have the spell wear off in the middle of the prom, leaving her stranded on the dance floor, doing the Funky Chicken in her jammies.

I know, it sounds ghastly to someone of your refined tastes. But remember, we're talking Hollywood here, the town that brought you *My Mother the Car* and *The Gong Show*. The head writers loved it! Okay, so maybe they didn't love it. But they liked it. Enough to invite me to be a "guest writer" on the show for a week. And here's the truly wonderful part. If they liked working with me, they were going to offer me a staff job! And if I did well on *Muffy,* it would be only a matter of time before I made the leap from syndication to prime time. Do you know how much prime-time sitcom writers make? Well, neither do I. But I hear it's scads. Truckloads of really big bucks. Think Bill Gates. Think Donald Trump. Think plumbers on overtime.

Ever since I'd handed in my script, I'd had visions of Seinfeldian contracts dancing in my head. I'd already mentally bought my beach house in Malibu, complete with his and hers Jaguars for me and my husband. Not that I had a husband, but I was sure I'd pick one up along the way.

All of which explains why I was in a jolly mood that morning as I drove past the wino sunning himself at the studio gates and onto the Miracle lot. I pulled up in front of the guard booth, where an ancient man with rheumy eyes and the unlikely name of Skippy asked me where I was headed.

"*Muffy 'n Me!*" I grinned.

Was it my imagination or did I see a trace of pity in those rheumy old eyes?

"Park over there," he said, waving to a tiny spot next to the commissary dumpster.

I parked my trusty Corolla in the shadow of the dumpster and stepped out onto the lot, trying to ignore the smell of rotting garbage. Swinging my brand-new attaché case, I headed over to the office I was to share with Kandi, eager to start on this exciting new chapter of my life. Somehow it still didn't seem real. I had to keep reminding myself that I actually had a job at Miracle Studios.

Of course, I didn't know it at the time, but the real miracle was that I'd live to tell about it.

Chapter Two

My friend Kandi has been a comedy writer, a waitress, and a part-time salesclerk at Bloomingdale's. But never as far as I know has she been a physician. Which is why, when I walked into her office that Monday morning, I was surprised to see her with a stethoscope dangling from her neck, the earpiece pressed up against the wall.

"What are you doing?"

"Listening to Stan and Audrey."

Stan and Audrey Miller were the head writers on *Muffy 'n Me*. I'd met with them when I first got my script assignment. They'd ushered me into their office and told me how much they'd liked my story outline, how the "Cinderella thing" really worked for them, and how they just wanted to suggest one or two teeny-tiny changes. Three hours later, they'd totally ripped my story apart and put it back together again. But I'd walked out with an assignment, and that was all I cared about.

Now here I was, in an office next to theirs, watching Kandi eavesdropping on them with a stethoscope.

"Where did you get that thing?" I asked.

"The prop department. It works like a dream. Want to try?"

"No, thanks. I prefer to do my eavesdropping at X-rated motels."

Kandi ignored my sarcasm.

"It's a great way to find out the latest dirt," she said. "Who's getting hired, who's getting fired. Who's getting laid."

"Well? What's happening?"

"Same old, same old. Audrey's accusing Stan of being an alcoholic, and he's accusing her of being a frigid bitch."

Apparently nobody was getting laid in that relationship.

Kandi took off the stethoscope and tossed it onto her desk.

"So," she said, gesturing around the room. "What do you think?"

Now I'm sure most people would assume that Hollywood sitcom writers have snazzy offices with plush carpeting and sleek teak furniture. Most people would be wrong. Kandi's office was a closet-sized affair, with stained brown carpeting and a dusty window overlooking the transvestites on Santa Monica Boulevard.

"Early Hellhole," I sighed, gazing at an ominous brown stain on the carpet. I didn't even want to *think* where that stain came from.

"That's your desk," Kandi said, pointing to a desk that was probably around in Fatty Arbuckle's day.

I was just about to plop down into the swivel chair in front of it when Kandi cried: "Stop!"

She reached into her drawer and pulled out a towel.

"Miracle Studios Rule Number One: Never Sit on Unprotected Furniture." She draped the towel on the chair seat. "I'm not kidding. The wardrobe lady swears she got a yeast infection from her chair."

I sat down gingerly and glanced over at a tennis racket propped up in the corner of the room.

"Do you actually have time to play tennis?"

"Nah. That's for scaring away the rats."

Obviously, this job was going to be a tad less glamorous than I'd thought.

Kandi took out her cosmetics case and started putting on lipstick without a mirror (along with comedy writing and making margaritas, one of her Major Life Skills).

"You ready for the big day?" she asked through puckered lips.

A frisson of fear shot through me. Today was the Monday morning read-through, a quaint sitcom ritual where the actors gather round, bleary-eyed from a weekend of debauchery, and read that week's script aloud for the first time. The script they were reading on that fateful Monday morning was my brilliant opus, "Cinderella Muffy."

Suddenly my palms glazed over with sweat. What if the actors didn't like it? What if nobody laughed? I'd once heard that back when Roseanne was doing her sitcom, she used to sit on the writers' scripts and fart! Good heavens! What if someone farted on my script? Or worse? I glanced down at the brown stain in the carpet and gulped.

My Malibu beach house fantasy instantly vanished, replaced by a Dickensian image of me back in my one-bedroom apartment, toiling away at a Toiletmasters brochure.

"Honey, are you okay?" Kandi ran a brush through her mane of enviably straight chestnut hair and gave her eyelashes a quick swipe with mascara.

"Oh, God," I wailed. "What if the actors don't like my script?"

Kandi snorted.

"Sweetie, they're *actors*. The ones with big parts will love it. The ones with small parts will think it 'needs work.'" She snapped her mascara wand back into its case. "Half of them don't even read the script. They just go through it with a marker and highlight their lines. If they don't see a lot of neon yellow on the page, they get pissy."

Her toilette complete, she reached for her copy of my script.

"Come on. We'd better head over to the stage, or we'll be late."

But by now I was frozen with fear in my vermin-infested chair.

"Come on, honey," she said, prying me up. "It won't be bad. I promise."

Then she led me out the door, a Hollywood lamb to the slaughter.

There are three things visitors to Los Angeles should avoid at all costs. Earthquakes. Freeways during rush hour. And the Miracle Pictures Studio Tour. A ninth-rate imitation of the Universal Studios Tour, the Miracle "tour" consisted of a ramshackle tram snaking its way past termite-ridden sets and an ancient roller coaster the Miracle bigwigs picked up cheap from a bankrupt amusement park.

As Kandi and I stepped out of the Writers' Building into the hazy sunshine, I could see the roller coaster in the distance. The unfortunate tourists strapped on board were screaming in genuine terror. I didn't blame them. The ride looked like it was made of popsicle sticks held together with Elmer's glue. Any minute now, the cable would probably snap like a worn-out rubber band.

And the pathetic thing is that I wished I was on it. At that moment, I wished I was anywhere else but on my way to the read-through. By now I was certain the actors would trash my script and blackball me from show biz forever. Heck, after word of my humiliation spread, I'd be lucky to get work from Toiletmasters.

"Will you please stop looking so terrified," Kandi said. "Everything's going to be great."

"Yeah, right. Just like everything was great when you booked us on that singles cruise to Cabo San Lucas."

Kandi sighed. "Are you never going to let me forget that? I've already apologized a gazillion times. How was I supposed to know it was a gay cruise?"

"You could've read the brochure, for starters."

"It wasn't so bad. You got hit on by some very attractive women."

At this point, my hysteria was interrupted by a Miracle Studios tram rattling past us. Unlike the roller coaster victims, the tram people were stifling yawns, clearly bored out of their skulls.

But when they saw Kandi and me, walking along with our scripts, they looked up with interest. It suddenly occurred to me that, to these people, we were glamorous. After all, we worked in Hollywood. They probably thought we hobnobbed with the stars, doing lunch with Julia and dinner with Brad.

By now, several of them were starting to wave. For a moment I forgot my terror and basked in their admiration. Maybe this Hollywood thing would work out after all. I smiled at their eager faces and waved back at them demurely, very Queen Elizabeth. Suddenly one of them shouted, "Hey, Vanessa! How's it going?" And I realized that they weren't waving at me, but at someone behind me.

I turned and saw the object of their adulation, Vanessa Dennis, the star of *Muffy 'n Me*. A startlingly lovely teenager, Vanessa had the face of an angel and the body of a Barbie doll. I strongly suspected that her breasts, like Barbie's, were of the man-made variety.

She clomped over to us on tottering heels, her endless legs encased in tight capri pants, her breasts spilling out from a halter top cut so low, it was practically a belt.

"Damn," Kandi muttered under her breath. "It's V.D."

"V.D.?"

"Vanessa Dennis. An affectionate nickname favored by all who know and loathe her."

Vanessa tottered toward us, ignoring her adoring fans in the tram.

"Watch," Kandi whispered. "She's going to ask me for a cigarette. Every week, she asks me for a cigarette. Every week, I tell her I don't smoke, and she still asks me for a cigarette."

Vanessa's breasts were soon at our side; seconds later, the rest of Vanessa showed up.

"Hi, Vanessa," Kandi said. "I'd like you to meet a friend of mine."

"Whatever," she said, not bothering to look at me. "You got a cigarette?"

"Sorry." Kandi smiled through gritted teeth. "I don't smoke. I may have mentioned that once or twice."

She turned to me. "How about you?"

"Sorry." I shrugged apologetically. "I don't smoke either."

With that, I ceased to exist for her.

"Christ," she moaned to Kandi. "Did you see this week's script? What a piece of crap. Who wrote this shit?"

I smiled weakly.

"That would be me."

"Oh, well," she said, not the least bit embarrassed. "Maybe they can fix it in rewrites." And with that, she hurried off in search of a cigarette.

"Now I know why they call her V.D."

"Don't pay any attention to Vanessa," Kandi said. "She hates all the scripts. Honest. She wouldn't know something funny if it bit her on the fanny. Which, rumor has it, is at least fifty percent foam rubber."

"She wears falsies on her tush?"

"Sure. Lots of actresses do."

I shook my head in amazement. I couldn't imagine someone actually wanting to increase the size of her butt, when I spent most of my waking hours wishing mine would disappear.

"Enough gossip," Kandi said. "It's show time." And with that she took me by the elbow and ushered me inside my first Hollywood soundstage.

I have to admit, I was impressed. At one end of the cavernous building were the *Muffy 'n Me* sets. I saw Muffy's cozy living room, her homey kitchen, and her Gidgetesque bedroom—complete with vanity table, lace curtains, and mountains of stuffed animals on her pink chenille bedspread. It was all just like I'd seen it on TV. Only here on the set, there were giant overhead lights, and the floor was crisscrossed with marking tape, to show the actors where to stand.

Across from the sets were the bleachers, where every week a bunch of unsuspecting tourists were herded in to witness the latest adventures of our gal Muffy. Between the two areas, where the cameras would later shoot all the action, a long metal conference table had been set up.

I gulped at the sight of it. In just minutes, I'd be seated at that table, listening to my script being read aloud for the first time.

"C'mon," said Kandi, "let's get some coffee."

She led me over to a buffet table laden with coffee, bagels, danish, and fruit.

"Kandi, I'm wired to the hilt as it is. If I have any coffee, I'll be bouncing from the ceiling."

"Cream or sugar?" she asked.

"Both," I sighed. "Extra sugar."

"How about a bagel?"

"Nah. Too fattening."

"There's the cream cheese."

"Thanks," I said, heaping some onto my bagel.

That's something you should know about me. I'm a lovely person, but a bit wanting in the willpower department.

"Okay," Kandi said, "let me fill you in on the cast of characters. You see that little guy over there. The one who looks like a Keebler elf?"

She pointed to a short guy in jeans and a sweatshirt, a too-small baseball cap perched on his head. He did look like a Keebler elf. Either that, or one of the Rice Krispies brothers.

"That's Alan Carlson, the director. The guy's been directing sitcoms forever. I think he started when Lucy was pregnant with Little Ricky. He's no Martin Scorcese, but he's fast and he's good.

"The big guy he's talking to is Marco, the prop man. If he looks a little frantic, it's because his wife is about to give birth any day now."

"Does Marco know you swiped his stethoscope?"

"No, and don't go blabbing."

"My lips are sealed."

"Vanessa, of course, you've met."

I looked over at where Vanessa was sitting at the conference table, fanning herself with my script. Oh, well. At least she wasn't sitting on it.

A young bronzed surfer dude was at her side, staring at her worshipfully.

"That's Zach Levy-Taylor."

I recognized him. "He's the kid who plays Muffy's boyfriend on the show."

"He'd like to be playing her boyfriend off the show, too," Kandi said, "but Vanessa won't give him a tumble."

Indeed, Zach was trying desperately to make conversation, but Vanessa barely glanced at him, concentrating instead on pushing back her cuticles.

"And that's Dale Burton, the actor who plays Muffy's dad."

She pointed to a J. Crewish-handsome man talking loudly into his cell phone.

"Dale's nuts. I know he looks as normal as apple

pie, but he's certifiable. You know who he's on the phone with?"

"Who?"

"Probably the recorded weather lady. Or the time-at-the-tone lady."

"But his lips are moving. He's talking."

"I know. He pretends to be talking to big show biz honchos. He wants everybody to think he's in demand."

"You're the greatest, Stevie Spielberg," I heard him shout into the phone. "Give my best to your lovely wife Kate."

"Quelle nutcase," I said.

Then Kandi caught sight of a petite woman with spikey orange hair. "That's Teri, the makeup lady. Hey, Teri," she called out. "You get my mascara?"

The orange pixie nodded, holding up a shopping bag.

"I'll be right back," Kandi said to me.

"Where are you going?" I asked, panicked. She wasn't going to leave me alone, was she?

"To pick up my mascara. Teri got it for me whole-sale. It's the same stuff Gwyneth Paltrow uses."

And before I could stop her, she was sprinting across the room, leaving me stranded at the coffee urn. Everybody around me was chatting it up, oozing camaraderie, and I just stood there, stuffing my face with empty calories. It was my sophomore year in high school all over again.

And then something happened that never happened in high school. A gorgeous guy walked up to me. Tall and rangy, with thick dark hair and startling green eyes.

"Hi," he smiled, revealing the most beautiful teeth I'd ever seen in my life. I honestly didn't know teeth could be that white.

I recognized him, of course. He was Quinn Kirkland, the actor who played Muffy's Uncle Biff.

Now usually in show biz, the gorgeous people aren't

funny. I mean, when was the last time you had a hearty chuckle over a Harrison Ford performance? But Quinn was a definite exception to this rule. From the episodes I'd seen, he was by far the funniest performer on *Muffy*.

"And who might you be?" he asked, still beaming his mega-watt smile.

Uh . . . wait. I know the answer to that. Just give me a minute.

"Jaine," I finally managed to blurt out. "Jaine Austen."

"Really?" he grinned. "I love your books."

I hear that line all the time. And usually I hate it. But coming from Quinn, it suddenly seemed quite amusing.

"It's Jaine with an 'i,'" I explained.

"I liked your script, Jaine-with-an-i," he said, almost blinding me with his smile.

"Thanks," I said, blushing furiously.

Good heavens. The man was *exceedingly* attractive. I could practically smell his pheromones in the air.

Quinn was obviously the kind of guy who left a trail of lovestruck women behind him. But I wasn't about to be one of them. No way. Dating an exceedingly attractive man is like going jogging without a sports bra. Sooner or later, you're bound to get hurt. Besides, I try never to date anyone who lookes better in a bathing suit than I do.

So I wasn't about to fall for a guy like Quinn Kirkland. Which is a good thing, because the next thing I knew, Quinn spotted Stan and Audrey Miller coming in the door and dropped me like a hot onion bagel.

"Sorry," he said, "but I've got to talk to some people who are more important than you."

Okay, so he didn't really say that.

What he really said was: "Nice talking to you." And then he proceeded to dash across the room to suck up to the Millers.

If I had to guess, I'd say Stan and Audrey were some-where in their forties. But I didn't have to guess, be-cause Kandi told me she'd looked up their ages on their W9 forms.

If ever there was a couple who didn't looked like they belonged together, Stan and Audrey were it. Audrey was reed thin and perfectly packaged—very Armani. Stan, on the other hand, was a pasty-faced guy with a sizable gut and a fondness for baggy sweats—very Pastrami.

I was standing there, nursing my coffee (I'd long since wolfed down my bagel) and watching Quinn flash his blinding smile at Audrey, when an elderly man with a thick mane of silver hair approached.

"Allow me to introduce myself," he said, with a vel-vety English accent. "I'm Wells Dumont."

"Of course I know who you are, Mr. Dumont. You play Muffy's neighbor, Mr. Watkins."

"I hear you're the writer of this week's delightful episode."

"Guilty as charged."

"It's really quite amusing. It has a charmingly fey quality that reminds me of Shakespeare's *Love's Labour's Lost.*"

Wow. The man was comparing me to Shakespeare! I couldn't wait to tell the guys at Toiletmasters about this.

"Are you familiar with the bard's comedies?" he asked hopefully.

"Not intimately, no."

"Oh."

He looked so disappointed, like a Jim Carrey fan in a roomful of Hegelian philosophers.

"But I like his other stuff," I said, trying to cheer him up.

"Really? What's your favorite Shakespearean play?"

"Uh . . . *Macbeth*," I said, pulling one out of thin air and praying he wouldn't ask me anything about it. Like, say, the plot.

His eyes lit up.

"Really? What a coincidence. It's my favorite, too. I've played the tortured thane many a time."

Tortured thane? What the heck was a thane? One of these days, I told myself, I really had to brush up on my Shakespeare. Just as soon as I finished my back issues of *Cosmo*.

"I've got a wonderful idea. Why don't I take you someplace where we can discuss our love of the bard over chilled martinis?"

Good heavens! The guy was old enough to be my really old father. Was he actually asking me out on a date?

"I know a charming French restaurant that serves the most wonderful *pommes frites*."

Sure sounded like a date to me.

"Well?" He smiled hopefully.

"Gee, I'd love to, but . . ."

But what? What was I going to tell him?

"But she's engaged to be married."

I turned to see Kandi back at my side. I shot her a grateful smile.

"Her fiance Duane is a great guy," Kandi said, "but terribly jealous."

"Lucky man," Wells said. He took my hand and kissed it. "A pleasure meeting you, my dear."

Then, undoubtedly brokenhearted, he headed over to the pastry tray to seek solace in a prune danish.

"Duane?" I whispered to Kandi. "My fiance's name is Duane?"

"You don't like it? Invent your own lovers."

By now, Audrey and Stan had wandered over to the conference table.

"Okay, everybody," Audrey called out, "let's get started."

Kandi and I took our seats at the table.

It was interesting to note that Audrey, not Stan, sat at the head of the table. Stan sat at her right hand, puffy and pasty-faced, taking occasional sips from an Evian water bottle.

Dale was still on the phone with his imaginary celebrity. "Gotta run, Antonio," he said, loud enough for everybody to hear. "Give my best to Melanie."

Kandi kicked me under the table and rolled her eyes.

"Before we start reading," Audrey said, "I'd like you all to meet the author of this week's script, Jaine Austen."

Quickly, before anyone could say, "Love your books," I added, "No relation."

Zach, the teenage adonis, looked up from where he was marking his script with a highlighter.

"No relation to who?"

Uh-oh. Not exactly the sharpest tool in the shed.

"Jeez," Vanessa sighed. "Don't you know anything? Jane Austen is a famous writer."

Zach's eager smile faded. "Oh."

"She wrote the movie *Clueless*."

I waited for someone to point out that Jane had been dead for almost two centuries, but obviously no one was willing to ruffle the star's feathers.

Audrey glanced over at the director. He took his cue.

"Here we go, folks," he said. "Act One. Fade In: Muffy's Bedroom—Day. . . ."

As Kandi predicted, the reading went well. People were actually laughing. Mostly at Quinn Kirkland's lines. Even the lines that weren't so funny got laughs when Quinn said them.

Vanessa didn't seem to mind that Quinn was getting all the laughs. I guess she'd quite wisely figured out that her talent lay not in her comedic abilities but in her amazing bustline. Dale, on the other hand, clenched his jaw at every laugh Quinn got. Clearly, the *Me* of *Muffy 'n Me* was feeling a tad threatened.

But that was his problem, not mine.

I was just happy nobody farted.

Chapter
Three

Never Get Attached to Your Jokes. That's the first thing you learn when you're a sitcom writer. Because, chances are, they're going to be rewritten.

The rewrite process, I was about to discover, was a ruthless affair. No joke was sacred. If it didn't work in rehearsal, it was gone. Even if it worked in rehearsal, but someone thought of something funnier in the rewrite session, it was gone. So if you ever decide to become a sitcom writer, remember to grow a very thick skin.

Luckily, a couple of my jokes had scored well in the read-through. So the process wasn't too excruciating. Besides, I was happy just to be there.

Kandi and I spent the rest of the day working on the script with Audrey and Stan. As I had observed earlier, Audrey was the undisputed captain of the *S.S. Muffy*. Who would have thought that a woman with Audrey's icy good looks could be funny?

Sitting across from her, I marveled at how thin she was. Everything about her was thin. Her legs, her waist, her hips—even her nostrils. The only thing that wasn't thin was her thick head of perfectly coifed blond hair. I could tell it was going to be a struggle not to hate her.

Audrey and Kandi were the ones coming up with the strongest jokes. I managed to get in a few gags here and there. As for Stan, he sat with his feet up on his desk, sipping from his Evian bottle, and reading *Variety*—the Pillsbury Doughboy gone Hollywood. Every once in a while, he'd toss out an idea, which Audrey would promptly ignore.

At about one o'clock, we sent out for lunch from a trendy bistro. Audrey ordered a Chinese chicken salad, Kandi ordered a tuna on whole wheat, and Stan—clearly not worried about his burgeoning waistline—ordered the steak with shoestring fries.

"And what will you have, Jaine?" Audrey asked, looking up at me over the rims of her five-hundred-dollar designer glasses. I scanned the menu, looking for something lo-cal. It was a toss-up between the nicoise salad and the fruit plate.

"I'll have the meatloaf platter."

What did I tell you? No willpower whatsoever. It's disgraceful, *n'est-ce pas?*

Stan looked at me with newfound interest. *Aha*, he seemed to be saying. *A fellow nosher.*

"Help yourself to something to drink from the refrigerator," Audrey said, as she phoned in our lunch order.

And that's where I made my big mistake. I got up and headed for the small refrigerator in the corner of the room.

"No!" Stan shouted.

Huh? Hadn't Audrey just told me to 'help myself'?

Stan smiled apologetically. "Not that refrigerator. Use the one in the kitchen."

Kandi jumped up.

"I'll show her where it is," she said, steering me out of the room.

"What was that all about?" I asked when we were in the hall. "What's he keep in that refrigerator, anyway? Cocaine?"

"Close," she said. "All those bottles of Evian you see him drinking?"

"Yeah?"

"They're not Evian. They're gin."

"But he was drinking that stuff at ten in the morning."

"I know. He's amazing, isn't he? I'm surprised his liver is still functioning. He usually manages to stay awake until about three. Then he starts nodding off. By five, he's snoring like a buzzsaw."

We got some real Evian water from the designated refrigerator and headed back to the office. I snarfed my lunch down in mere minutes. Almost as quickly as Stan polished his off. He offered me some of his fries, which I had every intention of refusing. I wish I had. They were much too salty.

When Audrey had managed to force down a few mouthfuls of her Chinese chicken salad, we went back to work. Sure enough, by three o'clock, Stan was dozing. By five, I got a bird's-eye view of his tonsils as he snored. Audrey finally swatted him with a rolled-up script.

"Wake up, Stan. We can't concentrate with all that racket."

"Sorry." He smiled sheepishly. "Guess I must've dozed off."

We worked until six, then sent the script off to be re-typed and distributed to the actors, so they could have a fresh batch of lines to complain about.

"Well, kiddo," Kandi said as we walked to our cars. "You survived the first day. It wasn't so bad, was it?"

And I had to admit, it wasn't.

"You want to grab a bite to eat?" I asked.

"I can't." Kandi's eyes danced with excitement. "I've got a date."

"Really? I didn't know you were seeing anybody."

"I didn't want to tell you. I didn't want to jinx it." She put her bag down on the trunk of her car and hugged me. "Oh, God, Jaine. This one is Mr. Right."

Kandi says that about every guy she dates. For a girl who grew up on the mean streets of New York, Kandi can be incredibly naïve when it comes to men. But she looked so darn happy, I didn't want to bust her bubble.

"So?" I asked, faking enthusiasm. "What's he like?"

"Wonderful!" she gushed, a fountain of hope springing eternal. "I'll tell you all about him tomorrow. I promise!"

And with that, she gave me a quick hug and got into her car.

I watched her drive away, hoping that this time Kandi's Mr. Right wouldn't turn out to be another Mr. Mistake. Then I stepped over a banana peel that had fallen from the commissary dumpster and opened the door to my Corolla. The studio was quiet. The roller coaster had long since shut down for the day. The terrified tourists whose screams had pierced the air were now safely ensconced in their hotel rooms, vowing never again to trust their travel agents.

It had been a rough day for all of us. And we all survived. But unlike the tourists, I had to do it all over again tomorrow.

The first thing I did when I got home that night was reach for my Prozac. No, I'm not on antidepressants (not yet, anyway). Prozac is my cat, a twelve-pound furball with the appetite of a longshoreman.

I found her in the bedroom, curled up on my best cashmere sweater.

"Where the hell have you been?" she said, glaring at me balefully. (Okay, so she didn't actually say that, but I knew that's what she was thinking.) Prozac was used to having me home all day, at her beck and call, feeding her snacks and rubbing her belly on demand. I'd explained to her that this show biz thing was my big break, that soon she'd be eating Bumblebee tuna in the Malibu sun, but I guess she'd been too busy licking her privates to pay any attention.

"Prozac, honey," I said, scooping her up in my arms. "Forgive me for leaving ooo home alone! Pweese? Pwetty pweese?"

She shot me a look that undoubtedly meant, "Will you stop that inane baby talk? I'm a cat. Not an infant. Now where's my dinner?"

I hustled into the kitchen and opened a can of Gourmet Fish Innards, which she inhaled in record time.

Then, to celebrate my first day on the job, I poured myself a tiny glass of chardonnay. Oh, who am I kidding? It was a jelly glass, and I filled it practically to the brim.

I brought my chardonnay into the living room, along with a Jumbo Jack I'd picked up on the way home, and settled down on my sofa to enjoy the view. Of course, the only view outside my living room window is the neighbor's azalea bush. But I don't mind. I like azaleas. I'd much rather watch them than the evening news.

I live in a one-bedroom apartment in the slums of Beverly Hills. Well, technically it's not a slum. Technically it's a pleasant, middle-class street dotted with duplexes and jacaranda trees and small yapping dogs who drive Prozac crazy. But compared to the mega-mansions north of Sunset Boulevard, it's a slum. Trust me on that one.

My apartment is the back unit of a 1940's duplex. It's got the original hardwood floors, the original tile-work—and the original plumbing. Which is why I'm on a first-name basis with the guys at Toiletmasters.

As I sat sipping my chardonnay and watching the azaleas, Prozac ambled over. Still hungry after her fishgut dinner, she leaped up on the coffee table and started nosing around my Jumbo Jack. I crumbled a few pieces of

the burger and put them on a napkin for her. She sucked
them up in a single gulp and wailed for more.

"That's it," I said. "No more. Absolutely not. You've
had enough."

She looked up at me with huge green eyes, doing her
best to look adorable.

"Forget it," I said. "I'm not changing my mind." Defiantly,
I grabbed the burger and took a bite.

She meowed piteously.

"Besides," I said, over her howls, "I'm hungry. All I
had for lunch today was a tiny nicoise salad."

She shot me a look that said, *Yeah, right, and I climbed
Mount Everest.*

It went on that way for a minute or two, Prozac staring at me and me trying to ignore her meows. You'd
have thought she hadn't eaten in days.

I caved in, of course. I always do. I gave her some more
burger and took what remained of the Jumbo Jack into
the bathroom, where I sat on the edge of the tub and ate
it in peace.

I was just licking the last of the ketchup from my fingers when I heard someone knocking at the front door.

It was my neighbor, Lance Venable.

Lance is a shoe salesman at Neiman Marcus, and he
looks the part: tall and slim, with narrow feet and a
headful of tight blond curls. We've never actually spoken about it, but I've always assumed that he's gay, an
assumption I made one night when I saw him kissing
another guy on his front steps.

The trouble with Lance is he's got x-ray hearing. I'm
not kidding. A dog barks in Pomona, and Lance hears
it. Needless to say, he hears everything that goes on in
my apartment. I listen to *Jeopardy,* and Lance shouts
out the answers. I peel an onion, and he cries. I gargle,
and he spits. All of which leaves a lot to be desired in
the privacy department. But on the plus side, he's a really nice guy who's been there for me when I need him.

"So?" he grinned. "How was your first day on the job?"

"Come on in, and I'll tell you all about it."

I poured him some wine, and we sat facing each other at opposite ends of the sofa, taking turns rubbing Prozac's belly while I gave him the highlights of my day.

"Vanessa Duffy wears falsies on her tush?" he said when I was through.

"It's only a rumor."

"Can I spread it?"

"Be my guest." I felt absolutely no loyalty to V.D. after what she'd said about my script.

Lance put down his wine and grinned, excited. "Guess what?" he said. "I've got a really terrific idea for a sitcom."

Uh-oh. Kandi warned me stuff like this would happen. Everyone in Los Angeles has an idea for a movie/sitcom/ game/talk show. Once people know you're in show business, they want to pitch it to you.

"Oh?" I said warily.

"About a bunch of people working in the shoe department of a high-end department store. Called *If the Shoe Fits.*" He beamed proudly. "Either that, or *There's No Business Like Shoe Business.*"

"Sounds great," I lied.

"I'm so glad you like it. Because I thought maybe we could work on it together."

Oh, God. A sitcom about feet. What had I gotten myself into?

"Well, actually, I'm pretty busy right now," I hedged.

"It won't take you long, I promise. I'll write the actual script, and all you have to do is throw in a few jokes." He smiled eagerly. "So how about it?"

"What are you, crazy? You think I want to sit around thinking up bunion jokes?"

Okay, I didn't really say that. What I really said was, "Sure."

What can I tell you? I'm just a gal who can't say no, except maybe to lo-fat rice cakes.

"That's great!" he said. "I'm going home right now and start writing!"

I waved feebly as he bounded out the door. Poor Lance. He had about as much chance of selling his show as I had of fitting into a size 4 dress.

So there you have it. My thrill-a-minute home life. Featuring a cat with an eating disorder and a neighbor in shoe biz. But hey, it could have been worse. A lot worse. I could have still been married to The Blob.

I call my ex-husband The Blob because that's what he was. The man was the original couch potato. His motto was *"Never put off for tomorrow what you can put off forever."*

I stayed with The Blob for three mind-numbing years, then filed for divorce. The Blob got custody of the remote, and I got custody of the bills. I moved out of the house we were renting in Mar Vista, the one with The Blob's car parked diagonally across our front lawn. Through a friend of Kandi's, I managed to find my cozy apartment in Beverly Hills, where I've been living happily ever after with Prozac and my dear friends Ben & Jerry.

Having drained the last drop of wine from my glass, I headed for my computer to check my e-mail. I found the usual assortment of cyberspace offerings: low mortgages, instant credit, and online porn. I was particularly intrigued by a headline that promised to increase my penis by at least two inches.

The only normal e-mails I got were two letters from my parents. And I use the word "normal" advisedly. My parents are anything but. Don't get me wrong. They're very sweet people and I love them to pieces, but they're never going to wind up on the cover of *Good Mental Health Magazine.*

Two years ago, they moved from my hometown of

Hermosa Beach, California, to Tampa, Florida. Now very few people in their right mind would move from Hermosa, one of the loveliest beach towns in the Western Hemisphere, to a state that has waterbugs the size of small poodles. But my mom wanted to be near the Home Shopping Club.

I'm not kidding. She dragged my father three thousand miles across country so she could be near a shopping channel. My mother is a television shopaholic. You know those ghastly T-shirts they sell in the middle of the night, the ones with sequinned tigers plastered across your boobs? My mom has seven of them. With matching capri pants. Not to mention a drawer full of cubic zirconia rings. And enough Capodimonte to open her own curio shop.

Daddy, thank goodness, doesn't stay up with Mom ordering rhinestone flip-flops in the middle of the night. That's because he's too busy ordering Turbo Steamers. My father's hooked on cooking appliances. My parents' kitchen is home to the Turbo Steamer, the Wonda-Roaster, the Jet Air Cooker, and everything Ron Popeil has ever made. My father's probably the only man in the world who shouts "Set It and Forget It!" during sex.

Yes, my parents are definitely a match made in merchandising heaven. But like I said, they're really very sweet, and I love them to pieces when they're not driving me crazy.

I thought about opening their e-mails, but it had been an exhausting day, and I didn't have the energy to read about my mother's latest cotton-poly acquisitions. I'd tackle their letters in the morning. Right now, all I wanted was a bath.

So I shut down the computer and headed for the tub, where I soaked for a good forty-five minutes, going over the events of the day.

Things hadn't gone badly, not badly at all. True, Vanessa had been a bitch. But everyone else had been very nice. Wells Dumont had gone out of his way to tell me he liked my script. And so had Quinn Kirkland, he of the dazzling smile. Good Lord, how did he get his teeth so white, anyway? Must be one of those whitening kits. I made up my mind to pick one up the next time I was at the drugstore.

When every last nerve ending had been beaten into submission and my body was as limp as linguini, I heaved myself out of the tub and into a cotton nightshirt. I made a halfhearted attempt at running a brush through my mop of curls, then gave up and plopped into bed. I lay there, my arms and legs spread out to the four corners of the bed, and sighed with pleasure. There were definite benefits to sleeping alone. And this was one of them. I spent the rest of the evening scraping the last shards of peanut butter from the bottom of a jar and watching an old Doris Day movie on AMC, Prozac napping on my belly. Absolute heaven.

Who needed men, anyway? As somebody much smarter than me once said (it was either Gloria Steinem or Ethel Mertz, I forget who): Men are like Xerox machines. They're good for reproduction, but that's about it.

Yeah, right. If I was so damn happy sleeping alone, why did I spend the rest of the night dreaming about being trapped in a bathtub with Quinn Kirkland?

YOU'VE GOT MAIL!

TO: Jausten
FROM: Shoptillyoudrop
SUBJECT: Have you met Kelsey Grammer?

Jaine honey, I still can't believe it! My daughter, a sit-com writer! Have you met Kelsey Grammer yet? I hear he's much thinner in person.

I've told everybody at the condo complex how you're writing for *Buffy the Vampire Slayer*. By the way, my neighbor Edna's nephew lives out in L.A. Should I give him your number? I thought I'd ask first. I know how touchy you got when I gave your phone number to that fellow I met in the Home Shopping chat room. Really, darling, I had no idea he was writing from prison. Anyhow, let me know if you want to go out with Ernie Lindstrom (that's Edna's nephew's name). I think Edna said he was a fireman. Either that, or he just got fired. I forget which. Whatever he does, I'm sure he's a lovely fellow. Edna assures me he shows no signs of the schizophrenia that runs in his family.

Everything's fine here in Tampa. Well, not really. Actually, I've been worried about Daddy. He's been acting very strange lately. Even stranger than usual. Yesterday on my way to my Jazzercise class, I could have sworn I saw him following me in his car. Oh, well. Maybe I was just imagining it.

Anyhow, I bought the most fabulous simulated emerald and cubic zirconia ring last night. A $300 value, for only $49.95! Honestly, dear, you can't beat the bargains on TV. I wish you'd let me order you something. I saw the most adorable sequinned blazer the other day. It's a genuine Ralph Loren. Perfect for your exciting new life in show biz.

And speaking of show biz, you're not the only one hobnobbing with celebrities. Guess who moved into the complex? John Koskovalis! Well, that's about it, honey. Knock 'em dead at the studio. And if you run into the gal who plays Ray's wife on *Everybody Loves Raymond*, tell her I think she's adorable!

Love from,
Mom

TO: Shoptillyoudrop
FROM: Jausten
SUBJECT: It's Muffy, not Buffy

Hi, Mom—

I hate to break it to you and the gang at Tampa Villas, but I'm not working on *Buffy the Vampire Slayer*. My show is called *Muffy 'n Me*. And no, I haven't met Kelsey Grammer or the gal who plays Ray's wife on *Everybody Loves Raymond*. But if I should ever run into them, I'll be sure and give them your best.

Whatever you do, do *not* under any circumstances give my phone number to Edna's nephew. And thanks for the offer, but I think I'll pass on the sequinned blazer. A genuine Ralph Loren, huh? Any relation to Sophia?

Hugs & kisses,
Jaine

PS. Who the heck is John Koskovalis?

TO: Jausten
FROM: Daddyo
SUBJECT: Hi, Angel Cakes!

Hi, Angel Cakes!

How're things in Lala land? Mom tells me you've met Kelsey Grammer. Wow!

Last night I cooked a 7-pound chicken in just 20 minutes with my new Acu-Pressure cooker. It was quite delicious, once we scraped it off the ceiling.

Lots of kisses from your loving,
Daddy

PS. By the way, your mom is having an affair with one of the hosts from the Home Shopping Channel. Some slimeball by the name of John Koskovalis.

Chapter Four

I tried to look blasé, but I was as excited as a tourist from Des Moines. I was about to have my first lunch at the studio commissary.

I was so excited, in fact, I'd almost forgotten about that bizarre e-mail from Daddy. I suppose I should have been worried, but I wasn't. Somehow I couldn't picture my mother having an affair. It was like picturing Betty Crocker in a bikini. My father had to be wrong. He'd probably gotten some crazy notion in his head, like the time he was convinced our gardener was stealing lemons from our lemon tree. It turned out he was totally wrong. It was our neighbor who was stealing the lemons. So I suppose Daddy wasn't *totally* wrong; after all, some-one *was* stealing our lemons. But the gardener was blameless. Just as blameless, I was convinced, as my mother.

Which is why I barely gave Daddy's e-mail a second thought at work that day.

Kandi and I had spent the morning with Audrey and Stan, going over next week's script, a stirring opus called "Muffy's Revenge," all about what happens when Muffy turns her biology teacher into a frog.

As Kandi explained to me, sitcom writers often work on two scripts at once: the one they're shooting that week, and the one they're prepping for the following week. Frankly, I'd been relieved to be off the hot seat and slashing somebody else's script to shreds. And now we were taking a well-earned lunch break at the commissary.

I'd read all about the studio commissaries of Hollywood's golden age, deluxe eateries where mega-stars like Clark Gable and Joan Crawford mixed and mingled over Cobb salad. So you can imagine my disappointment when Kandi led me into the Miracle commissary, a shabby barn of a building with wobbly tables and scarred metal chairs. Because only two shows were in production on the lot (*Muffy 'n Me* and a show about a bunch of lady cops called *PMS Squad*), the commissary was fairly empty.

Quinn Kirkland, recent co-star of my x-rated bathtub dream, was sitting at a corner table with Wells Dumont and Dale Burton.

"Where's Vanessa?" I wondered.

"Oh, V.D. never eats with the commoners," Kandi said. "She usually stays in her dressing room, sharpening her fangs."

"Hey, ladies," Quinn called out when he saw us. "Come sit with us!"

Was it my imagination, or was he directing his heart-melting gaze at *moi*?

"We'll be right there," Kandi said, "as soon as we get our lunches."

Kandi led me over to a dingy steam table, manned by a woman with frizzled gray hair trapped in a hairnet. Her name tag read "Helga." A cigarette dangled from her lips, periodically dropping ashes into Today's Special. Clearly, Helga had not been informed that smoking was illegal in California eating establishments.

"What'll it be, gals?" she croaked in a raspy voice.

The menu was straight out of *Oliver Twist*. Today's

Special was something optimistically called London Broil. It looked more like recycled tires to me.

"Better stick with the sandwiches," Kandi whispered. "They come wrapped in cellophane. Guaranteed ash-free."

"I guess I'll have a sandwich," I said.

Helga scratched her none-too-clean hair through her hair net.

"What kind?" she asked. "Brown or white?"

"Brown or white?"

"White's cheese. Brown's meat."

"What kind of meat?"

"Beats me."

For once in my life, I'd lost my appetite.

"I'll have the cheese, I guess."

"How about you, toots?" she asked Kandi.

"What the heck? I'll go for brown."

"Are you sure you know what you're doing?" I whispered.

"It's safe," Kandi assured me. "They buy the sandwiches at a supermarket."

The old crone tossed us our sandwiches, and two cans of Diet Coke, and we joined the others.

Wells stood up as we approached the table, ever the courtly Brit.

"So nice to see you again, my dear," he said to me, patting the empty seat next to him.

Oh, great. I dream of hot sex in a bathtub with Quinn and wind up with the Geritol Kid. I smiled weakly and sat next to him. Kandi, lucky lady, managed to snag a seat next to Quinn.

Dale Burton had his cell phone out on the table. We'd probably just missed a call from Tom Hanks.

"So, how are you enjoying your first few days on the Miracle lot?" Wells asked.

"It's all very exciting," I said, looking down at the

greasy blobs of mayonnaise oozing out from my white sandwich.

"And how do you like our gourmet commissary?" Quinn asked with a grin.

He winked at me, and to my horror, I found myself blushing. What the heck was wrong with me? I was so damn flustered I could barely eat my sandwich, which wasn't all that surprising, since the cheese had the consistency of spandex leggings.

Oh, well. At least this was one meal where I wouldn't be stuffing my face. And then a wonderful thought occurred to me. If I ate at the commissary every day and the food was always this awful, I'd probably wind up losing tons of weight. By the end of the season I'd be Ally McBeal thin, thin enough to be dating a hunk like Quinn Kirkland. Who knew? Maybe we'd wind up deliriously in love. (Yes, I know I'd sworn off exceedingly attractive men, but Quinn was so *exceedingly* exceedingly attractive, I couldn't help myself.) I let my mind wander a tad and was just saying "I do" to Quinn in a beachside wedding ceremony, when my reverie was interrupted by the arrival of Marco, the prop guy.

"Hey, kids. Guess what I brought." He held up a six-pack of beer. "Dessert!"

Everybody cheered as he handed out the beers.

"How about you, Jaine?" Quinn asked. "You want one?"

Absolutely not. No way. If I wanted to wind up looking like Ally McBeal, the last thing I needed was a fattening beer.

"Sure. I'd love one," were the words that actually came out of my mouth.

"So how's your wife doing?" Kandi asked Marco.

"She's in much better shape than I am. I'm a nervous wreck."

I remembered what Kandi had told me, that Marco's wife was about to give birth any day now.

"Let's hear it for the papa-to-be," Quinn said, holding his beer can aloft in a toast.

"To the papa-to-be!" everyone said.

The beers were definitely the highlight of the meal. Before long, we were all sitting around companionably, chewing the fat like long-lost friends.

Quinn looked around the nearly empty commissary. "This place reminds me of a dive I used to work at when I was trying to break into the business. It was one of those steak-and-salad-bar steak houses. The chef was a crazy drunk. He used to squeeze the steaks under his armpit before he tossed them on the grill."

"Euuuu!" we all shrieked.

"That's nothing," said Marco. "I once worked on a show where the leading lady was such a bitch, she demanded a kosher pickle at every lunch. But it had to be a special pickle, from a deli all the way out in Tarzana. The propmaster hated her so much that every day before handing her the pickle, he used to piss on it."

Before long everyone was swapping Breaking Into Showbiz stories.

"When I worked as a waiter," Dale said, "we used to put phony names down on the reservations list. Names like 'Seymour Butt' and 'Tayka Leak.' The poor hostess would run around calling out, 'Tayka Leak! Is anyone here from the Tayka Leak party?'"

Quinn told about how, when he used to work as a valet parker in a swanky Malibu restaurant, he'd leave crazy things in the customers' glove compartments. One time he put a pair of black lace panties in a married couple's car. Another time, a snake. And another time, a week-old chili dog. Kandi told about her adventures writing one-liners for a sleazy comedian who tried to pay her off in postage stamps. And Wells told about the time he accidentally gave Lady Macbeth a wedgie.

The stories were great, and the laughter was contagious. No wonder people were always trying to claw their way into show business. It was so much damn fun.

Yet underneath all the hilarity, there was an unspoken competition to be the funniest. It was a contest, all right—subtle but undeniable.

And the winner was Quinn Kirkland. Just as at yesterday's read-through, Quinn was getting the biggest laughs. The interesting thing was that his stories weren't any funnier than anybody else's. But he had a way of telling them that made them seem hilarious. I don't know what it was—his timing, his expressiveness, or maybe just his amazing teeth. But whatever it was, it worked.

I looked around the room as everyone whooped with laughter at one of his adventures.

Everyone except Dale, who sat smiling stiffly, his jaws clenched like a vise.

"Yikes," Kandi said, looking at her watch. "It's after two."

We'd totally lost track of the time. Which is what happens, I guess, when you have beer for dessert.

The guys hurried off to the stage, and Kandi and I made our way back to the Writers' Building. I have to confess, I was feeling *tres* virtuous. I'd barely touched my rubber sandwich, which meant all I'd had for lunch was a 150-calorie beer. If you don't count the teeny-tiny bag of potato chips that I snagged on my way out of the commissary.

Yes, I was feeling pounds lighter already, only faintly aware of my thighs flapping together as we hurried across the lot.

We grabbed our copies of "Muffy's Revenge" and dashed into Stan and Audrey's office, only to find the two of them in deep discussion with what looked like a college kid in a three-piece suit.

"Are you sure you want to do this?" Stan was saying, as we burst in the room.

"I'm sure," the kid said.

Audrey looked up at us, irritated. We'd obviously shown up at a crucial moment in the conversation.

"Sorry to interrupt," Kandi said.

"We'll call you when we're ready for you," Audrey snapped.

We backed out the door, like geishas in a tearoom.

"Who was the kid in the suit?" I asked when we were back in our office.

"Jim Samuels. Programming exec at the network."

"That kid is a network executive?" I asked, gazing out the window at the transvestites on Santa Monica Boulevard. "He looks like he still needs somebody to cut his meat for him."

"In television, the kids are in control," Kandi said. "The logic is that only kids understand what other kids want to watch. And since the target age for most network shows is eighteen to thirty-four-year-olds, there are an awful lot of kids running the show. Everyone in TV is under thirty-five, and if they're not they lie about their age. Luckily for us, *Muffy* is considered so un-hip that the age thing isn't a huge issue."

Good Lord. At thirty-six years old, I was already prehistoric.

"Something's about to hit the fan," Kandi said, reaching into her drawer and taking out her stethoscope. "The network guys never show up unless there's trouble."

She put on the stethoscope and pressed the earpiece to the wall.

Across the street a black transvestite with a blond afro hopped into a Volvo station wagon with a guy who looked like a charter member of the Young Republicans.

Kandi started giving news bulletins from the wall.

"Jim's saying he's testing poorly with the target demographics."

"Who's testing poorly?"

"I don't know," she said, shushing me.

"Now Stan's saying, *How are we going to get rid of him?*

"And Audrey's saying, *As soon as his contract comes up for renewal, we can kill him off in a tragic automobile accident.*

"The network guy's saying, *Yes, and we can turn it into a lesson about the dangers of drunk driving.*

"And Audrey's saying, *And then Uncle Biff can adopt Muffy.*

"And now Jim's saying, *Let's do lunch sometime.*"

Kandi turned to me, the stethoscope dangling from her neck.

"They're talking about Dale. They obviously want to kill him off. And have Quinn take his place as Muffy's dad."

Just then I heard something rattling in the bushes outside Stan and Audrey's office.

"I wonder what Dale's going to do when he finds out," Kandi said.

"Come see for yourself."

"What are you talking about?"

I motioned her to my side and pointed to a figure crouched in the bushes, listening intently to every word of Stan and Audrey's conversation.

It was the future accident victim himself, Dale Burton.

As it turns out, what Dale did was dust himself off and slink out of sight.

"What a desperado," Kandi said. "I can't believe the man would hide in the bushes to eavesdrop."

"Look who's talking," I said, pointing to the stethoscope still dangling from her neck.

She had the grace to look marginally ashamed.

At which point, the phone rang. It was Audrey, summoning us back to rewrite duty. The Millers said nothing to us about Dale's imminent demise. Instead, we went back to work on next week's script as if no funeral bells were about to toll in Muffyland.

By four o'clock, Stan was well into his third Evian bottle of the day. So I was shocked when, in spite of enough gin in his veins to keep a bunch of fraternity boys drunk for a week, he actually managed to come up with an idea.

If you remember (and there are demerits for those of you who don't), the script we were working on was the stirring saga of what happens when Muffy turns her biology teacher into a frog. In the script, Muffy keeps the frog in her kitchen sink. Stan suggested that when Muffy's spell finally wore off, the audience would see the teacher, soaking wet, sitting crammed into Muffy's kitchen sink. Okay, so it wasn't Neil Simon, but it was an idea, one of Stan's very few.

"Not bad, Stan," Audrey said.

Stan beamed like a kid getting a gold star from his kindergarten teacher. It was pathetic how much he seemed to need Audrey's approval.

"Let's go down to the set," Audrey said, "and see if it's possible for someone to actually fit in the sink."

And so the four of us went trooping over to the stage, where Audrey was annoyed to see that the actors had already left for the day.

"It's like The Actors Country Club around here," she muttered. "I suppose we ought to be grateful that they put in an appearance each day."

Somewhere off in the distance, we heard a radio tuned to a Latin salsa station.

"Must be one of the crew," Stan said.

"At least somebody's working," Audrey sniffed, as she led us over to the kitchen set.

"Okay, Stan," she said, pointing to the sink. "Hop in."

"Me? Why me?"

"Because we need a man-sized butt. And when last I looked you were the only man in the room."

She shot him a look of steel. But surprisingly enough, Stan stood his ground.

"I'm not getting in there. You know I've got a bad back. Why can't one of the girls do it?"

Audrey turned and looked at us appraisingly. Kandi, with her size 6 tush, was quickly eliminated. Audrey gave my derriere the once-over. Apparently, it met her standards for a man-sized butt.

"Jaine," she smiled icily, "would you mind?"

"Of course I'd mind. That sink doesn't look big enough to hold a crockpot. The last thing I want to do is humiliate myself by trying to jam my butt into it."

Okay, so I didn't really say that. What I said was, "No problem."

I hauled myself up onto the kitchen counter, beginning to wonder if that beach house in Malibu was worth it. *Dear God,* I prayed as I lowered my butt into the sink, *please let it fit.*

And, I'm happy to report, it did.

Thank you, God, I said wordlessly. *Thank you thank you thank you thank you thank you—*

Then, somewhere around the seventh thank-you, I began to hear a faint groaning sound.

"What's that noise?" Audrey asked.

Oh, good Lord. The sink was about to collapse. It would be all over the studio by tomorrow: Jaine Austen sat in Muffy's sink and broke it! This would be the most humiliating event of my life. I could see the headlines in *Variety*. *Big Butt Sinks Sink!*

The groaning grew louder now, and I scrambled to get out of the sink before any more damage was done.

"It's coming from over there," Audrey said, pointing down to the other end of the stage.

Flooded with relief, I realized Audrey was right. The groaning wasn't coming from the sink, after all.

I lowered myself back onto terra firma and followed the others as Audrey led the way to the other end of the stage.

As we walked, the sounds of the salsa music grew louder. And it soon became clear that the groans were not coming from an inanimate object, but from a human being: A man, in the throes of passion. We walked past the living room set, down to where Muffy's bedroom was nestled in a remote corner of the stage. As we got closer to the bedroom, we could hear the breathy whimpers of a woman in ecstasy.

We peeked around the wall separating Muffy's bedroom from the living room set.

And there on top of the pink chenille bedspread, surrounded by an audience of stuffed animals, Quinn Kirkland was doing to Vanessa Duffy what the network was about to do to Dale Burton.

Chapter
Five

Talk about your embarrassing moments. What exactly are you supposed to do when you walk in on two people boffing like crazed rabbits? The only polite thing to do, I guess, is walk back out again. But we all just stood there, frozen, staring at Quinn's tanned tush as it bobbed up and down on top of Vanessa like an overheated piston.

Vanessa lay there, her long blond hair splayed out on the pillow, moaning in what I suspected was fake ecstasy. I don't know about you, but the last time I was in the throes of passion (some time in the McKinley administration), I didn't lie there with my eyes wide open staring at the ceiling. Which is what Vanessa was doing. Oh, sure, she was moaning stuff like *Oh, Quinn, baby, give it to me*, but I had the feeling it was just another acting job, and not a very good one at that.

Somewhere in the middle of her performance, her eyes wandered over in our direction.

"Oh, shit," she said. "We've got company."

Quinn looked over his shoulder and saw the four of us standing at the foot of the bed. He was uncomfortable for about a nanosecond; then he quickly regained his composure.

"Guess that's a wrap, Vanessa," he said, climbing off

her perfect body and reaching for his briefs, not the least bit perturbed.

"Quinn!" Audrey gasped. "How could you?"

There was something about the way she said it, her voice husky with emotion, that roused my suspicions. Call me crazy, but she sounded a lot more like a betrayed lover than a disinterested head writer. Was it possible, I wondered, that Audrey had been having an affair with Quinn?

Quinn shrugged lazily. "Sorry, babe," was all he offered by way of an explanation.

Audrey turned and marched out of the sound stage, her heels clicking angrily. Stan hurried after her.

I stood gawking, like a witness at the scene of an auto accident. Kandi grabbed me by the elbow and led me away. I turned back one more time to look at Quinn, zipping up his jeans. And to my utter amazement, he winked at me. Good Lord. He'd just finished boffing Vanessa, was possibly screwing Audrey, and now he was flirting with me. The man had the scruples of a gnat.

At that moment my Quinn fantasies bit the dust. I didn't care how dazzling his smile was; the last thing I needed was an amoral sexaholic who had no qualms about sleeping with a minor. I was definitely going to have to kick him out of my Malibu beach house and find someone new to marry.

Kandi was strangely silent on our way back to the Writers' Building. I thought she'd be bubbling over with excitement at the giant nugget of gossip that had just been dropped in our laps. But she said nothing, just marched ahead grimly, her script clutched tightly to her chest.

"Kandi, is anything wrong?"

"Yes," she said, her voice catching.

It was then that I noticed two teardrops oozing out from the rims of her sunglasses.

"What is it?" I asked.

"Remember the guy I told you about yesterday? The one I was so crazy about?"

"Oh, God. It's not Quinn, is it?"

She nodded.

"We've been seeing each other for the past month."

By now she was openly crying, tears streaming down her face, snot running from her nose.

"I've got to get a grip," she said, wiping her nose with her sleeve. "I can't let Stan and Audrey see me this way."

But she needn't have worried, because just then Audrey came storming out of the Writers' Building, followed by a bewildered Stan. The two of them got in their matching Mercedes and drove off the lot in a cloud of expensive exhaust fumes.

"You know what you need right now?" I said.

"Intravenous doses of Zoloft?"

"You need a nice frosty margarita."

She smiled wanly. "That does sound nice."

Fifteen minutes later we were seated across from each other inhaling egg rolls and margaritas in a cozy booth at the Formosa Café. The Formosa is a popular Hollywood watering hole with worn leather booths and 8x10 glossies of long-dead celebrities hanging over the bar.

"He told me he wanted to marry me," Kandi said, stirring her margarita morosely.

"He did?"

"Well, he said someday he hoped we could be together. Isn't that the same thing?"

"No, Kandi," I sighed. "It's not the same thing. When a man wants to marry someone, he says, *Will you marry me?* When he wants to get in a woman's pants, he says, *Some day I hope we can be together.*"

"He said we could move in together as soon as his divorce was final."

"His divorce? Don't tell me he's married!"

"Separated. His wife lives in Manhattan. They haven't gotten along for years."

"Or so he says. He could be flying back east and boffing her on the weekends for all you know."

"No, he couldn't be. He's been with me every weekend."

"He has?"

"Not every weekend," she admitted. "But a lot of them. Well, one or two, anyway." She took a mournful slurp of her margarita and sighed. "And all the while I thought he loved me, he's probably been screwing V.D."

"Actually, Kandi, I think he may have been having a thing with Audrey, too."

"Audrey?" Kandi's eyes widened with disbelief.

"Didn't you see the look on her face when she saw him in bed with Vanessa?"

"No." Kandi sniffled. "I was too busy trying not to cry."

"It was definitely the face of a woman scorned. She was pissed to beat the band."

"I don't believe it," she said, shaking her head, stunned. "V.D. *and* Audrey?"

Needless to say, I didn't tell her about the blinding smiles Quinn had been flashing in my direction. Why make her even more miserable than she was already?

"That does it," she said, angrily spearing an egg roll. "I've had it with men. From now on I'm going to lead a sexless monastic existence, like Mother Teresa. And you."

"Gee, thanks."

"Well, you have to admit, you haven't exactly been burning any mattresses lately."

She had a point there. The only men in my boudoir of late had been Mr. Clean and Mr. Bubble.

"Another round?" she asked.

"I can't," I said. "I'm teaching my class tonight."

"Oh, right. It's Tuesday. I forgot. Guess I'd better get the bill."

She signaled the waiter for the check.

"Gosh," she said, flustered. "How embarrassing."

"What?"

"When I waved at the waiter, some guy at the bar thought I was waving at him. And now he's waving back at me."

I looked over and saw a tall, sandy-haired guy in tight jeans leaning against the bar, smiling at us.

"He's sort of cute, isn't he?" Kandi whispered.

Some people never learn.

Chapter
Six

It turned out that the cute guy in tight jeans was waiting at the bar for his date, another cute guy in tight jeans. Kandi and I paid the check and headed out to the parking lot.

"Want me to call you later?" I asked.

"Nah, that's okay. I'll be fine."

I gave her a hug, and waved as she drove off in her Miata. I wasn't really worried about her. I knew she'd be okay. Kandi has an amazing ability to rebound from failed relationships. Comes from years of practice, I guess.

Most of the time I'm glad I'm not Kandi. I'm glad I'm not taking chances and getting hurt. But every once in a while, when I'm lying in bed, watching old Lucy reruns in the middle of the night, with only my cat for company, I wonder if Kandi isn't the smart one, after all. At least she's trying.

I got into my Corolla and headed across town to the Shalom Retirement Home, where once a week I teach a class in memoir writing. Sad to say, I have no budding Mary Karrs or Frank McCourts in my class. Most of my students' essays tend to be about things like *My Granddaughter's Bat Mitzvah* or *My Son, the Orthodontist.* Every once in a while I'll get something spicier like *My*

Son Married a Shiksa, but that's about as compelling as it gets.

But they're a lively bunch, and I get a kick out of them. Most of them are in their eighties and many of them have never written before. It's not easy to write at any age, let alone to start when you're an octogenarian. In spite of their many infirmities, they're still giving life a shot. And for that, I admire them.

I inched across town in heavy traffic, cursing my fellow drivers, especially the ones with cell phones glued to their ears.

When I finally showed up, ten minutes late for class, I was greeted by a round of applause from the handful of students gathered in the Shalom rec room. Ever since I'd told them about my job on *Muffy 'n Me*, they'd been treating me like Hollywood royalty.

"Author, author!" shouted Mrs. Pechter, a sweet woman with bosoms the size of throw pillows.

"We're so proud of you, darling," chimed in tiny, birdlike Mrs. Rubin. "Imagine! Our teacher, a famous TV writer."

"Wait a minute," I said. "I'm not famous yet."

"But you will be," said Mrs. Rubin. "Just like the famous playwright Wendy Wasserman."

"It's not Wasserman," said Mr. Goldman, the only man in the class. "It's Wasserstein."

"My son's wife went to school with Wendy Wasserstein," Mrs. Zahler announced.

"That's nothing," Mr. Goldman countered. "My cousin Mel once dated Neil Simon's mother-in-law."

"Are you sure her name isn't Wasserman?" Mrs. Rubin asked. "I could've sworn it was Wasserman."

That's how conversations go at the Shalom Retirement Center.

"Okay, class!" I said. "Let's get started, shall we? Who wants to read what they wrote this week?"

"So tell me," Mrs. Pechter said, unwilling to let go

of show biz, "what's Wells Dumont really like? I saw him in a play once. Something by Shakespeare, I think. Such a handsome man."

"Feh," opined Mrs. Rubin. "He's nothing compared to Quinn Kirkland. What a doll."

The other ladies nodded in agreement.

"So what's Quinn like?" Mrs. Zahler asked. "He a friendly sort of fellow?"

If they only knew.

"Yes." I managed to restrain myself. "Quinn Kirkland is quite friendly, indeed."

"And how about Vanessa Duffy?" Mr. Goldman asked, with a wink. "You think maybe she likes older men?"

He wasn't kidding. A retired carpet salesman with enough chutzpah to fuel a space ship, Mr. Goldman only had eyes for women young enough to be his grand-daughters. Like, for instance, me. For years, Mr. Goldman had been trying to get me to go out on a date with him. And for years, I'd been turning him down, a fact which didn't seem to discourage him. Yes, if there was one fly in the Shalom ointment, it was Mr. Goldman.

I was grateful that Vanessa seemed to have supplanted me as the object of Mr. Goldman's affections. Maybe this meant he'd leave me alone and quit asking me to go for moonlight strolls in the Shalom parking lot.

"So how about it?" he asked, his dentures twinkling merrily. "You think Vanessa would go for a guy like me?"

"You'll find out on Friday," I said.

I'd arranged for the class to be in the audience for the taping of my show. I figured a few loyal fans couldn't hurt. And they were overjoyed at the prospect of being show biz insiders.

"I can't wait," Mrs. Rubin said. "Imagine. My first TV taping."

"Big deal," Mr. Goldman said. "I've been to plenty of TV tapings. I saw *Laverne & Shirley.* I saw *Blansky's*

Beauties. I saw *Joanie Loves Chachi*. That Joanie. What a doll. She had the warmies for me."

The ladies groaned.

"As if," Mrs. Pechter muttered, a phrase she'd no doubt picked up from her granddaughter's bat mitzvah.

"Hey, I've got a great idea for a sitcom," Mr. Goldman continued, ignoring his detractors. "They should do a show about me. I'm just as funny as that Seinfeld guy. Funnier, probably."

"My cousin went to high school with Jerry Seinfeld's mother."

"Really? My brother-in-law once dated Joan Rivers."

"Class!" I called out. "Maybe we could get started now."

"They could call it *Goldman*. It would be all about my life in the carpet business. Maybe they could get Heather Locklear to play my girlfriend."

"My daughter goes to Heather Locklear's gynecologist."

I sat back and sighed.

We never did get to read any essays that night.

YOU'VE GOT MAIL!

TO: Daddyo
FROM: Jausten
SUBJECT: What on earth?

What on earth makes you think Mom is having an affair?

TO: Jausten
FROM: Daddyo
SUBJECT: Wake up and Smell the Coffee
Oh, come on, Sweetpea. I didn't just fall off a turnip truck. I've seen enough *Oprah* to know when a woman's cheating. Mom's showing all the classic signs. She's losing weight, she's getting her teeth capped. She's taking showers. Lots and lots of showers. She's got something cooking on the back burner, all right, and I know who it's with. That greaseball from the shopping channel. I saw them together in the clubhouse the other morning, making serious eye contact. He pretended he was giving her his autograph, but my bet is that they were making plans for a secret rendezvous.

TO: Shoptillyoudrop
FROM: Jausten
SUBJECT: What the heck is going on?

Daddy says you're having an affair with that Koskovalis guy from the Shopping Channel. He says you've lost weight and are having your teeth capped and taking an inordinate number of showers.

What the heck is going on???

TO: Jausten
FROM: Shoptillyoudrop
SUBJECT: The Deep End

This time, your father has definitely gone off the deep end. I am NOT having an affair with John Koskovalis! Good heavens, I've only met the man once, at the clubhouse. I asked him for his autograph, and he gave it to me. End of story.

And as for those other accusations, just because I've joined a Jazzercise class and lost a few pounds and decided to make a lifelong dream come true by having my teeth capped, that doesn't mean I'm having an affair. And, yes, I'm taking a lot of showers. It gets sweaty at Jazzercise!

PS. Are you sure you don't want me to give your number to Ernie Lindstrom?

Chapter
Seven

News of the Vanessa/Quinn boff-a-thon spread through the studio like wildfire. Everyone was talking about it. On my way to my office the next morning, I saw Marco, the prop guy, huddled with Teri, the makeup lady.

"They had to send the bedspread to the dry cleaners," I heard Teri say.

"And one of the stuffed animals, too," Marco added.

Outside Stan and Audrey's office, their secretary, Bianca, was deep in conversation with Danny, the production assistant, whispering something about statutory rape.

No doubt about it; Quinn and Vanessa were definitely the topic du jour. I wouldn't have been surprised if the hookers on Santa Monica Boulevard knew about their fling.

Kandi was already in our office when I got there, sitting slumped behind the desk, pale and puffy-eyed.

"How's it going, kiddo?" I asked.

"Quinn called me last night. At eleven o'clock. Wanted me to come over."

"You didn't, did you?"

"No, uh . . . of course not," she stammered.

I shot her a look.

"Okay, I did, but just for a little while."

"Kandi, what am I going to do with you?"

"Don't worry. It's all over. He acted as if nothing had happened. When I asked him how he could cheat on me with Vanessa, he told me to grow up and stop acting like a baby. He actually expected me to hop into bed with him."

"Did you?"

"No way. That much of a masochist, I'm not."

"So what did you do?"

"The only dignified thing I could do. With my head held high, I walked out of his house, down his driveway, and wrote *Screw You* in lipstick on the windshield of his Porsche."

"That was taking the high road, all right."

"Hey, Quinn's lucky I didn't kill him. I sure would have liked to."

At which point we looked up and saw Bianca standing in the doorway. A sharp-faced young woman with small teeth and darting eyes, Bianca reminded me of a ferret named Freddy my sixth-grade class adopted as a science project.

Bianca had been Audrey's secretary for the past seven years. According to Kandi, Audrey had lured Bianca with vague promises of a writing assignment. But seven years later, Bianca was still answering phones and picking up Audrey's dry cleaning.

She was standing in the doorway now, fiddling nervously with a chopstick hair ornament that speared her dull brown hair in a French twist.

"Uh . . . hi, guys," she said, trying to pretend she hadn't been listening to our conversation. "I brought you the revised scripts."

Then, as quick as Freddy the ferret, she tossed us our scripts and scurried away, armed with fresh fodder for the gossip mill.

* * *

We spent the morning with Audrey and Stan, writing the teacher-in-the-sink scene. Audrey had totally regained her Ice Queen composure. Looking at her, you'd never guess that less than twenty-four hours ago, she'd been oozing fury. In fact, she was so cool and collected, I was beginning to wonder if maybe I'd been wrong. Maybe she hadn't been having an affair with Quinn. Maybe her anger yesterday was simply the anger of a head writer whose actors have been behaving badly.

But then I looked down and saw how tightly she was clutching her pencil, so tightly that the veins in her hand were standing up like mountain ranges on a relief map. And I figured maybe I hadn't been wrong after all.

And was it my imagination, or was Stan gulping down his Evian/gin even faster than usual? If Audrey had been having an affair with Quinn, did Stan know about it? Did he care? Or did they have one of those Don't Ask, Don't Tell relationships?

I could have gone on like that for hours, musing on the nature of their relationship, but there was a Malibu beach house at stake, so I forced myself to concentrate on the job at hand and think up some jokes for a teacher-cum-goldfish.

At noon we broke for lunch, and Kandi and I headed back to our office.

"Want to go to the commissary?" I asked.

"I can't face the commissary." Kandi sighed, stretching out on the filthy plaid sofa in our office. "I don't want to risk running into Quinn."

"Kandi!" I said, eyeing the sofa. "What are you doing? Aren't you going to cover it with a towel? What if you get a yeast infection?"

"Oh, who cares? I'm never going to have sex again anyway, so what does it matter?"

"You want me to get us some sandwiches?"

"I'm not hungry."

"C'mon, you've got to eat something."

"Okay, bring me a sandwich."

"Brown or white?"

"You choose."

I left her lying on the germ-infested sofa and made my way to the commissary.

Kandi needn't have worried; Quinn was nowhere to be seen. The commissary was practically deserted. The only people there were some extras in cop uniforms from *PMS Squad*, sitting at a table in the middle of the room. As I walked past their table, I heard one of them say, ". . . and she wrote *Screw You* on his windshield with her lipstick."

Wow. When it came to news dissemination, this place was faster than CNN.

I got two brown sandwiches from Helga the Sandwich Nazi and headed out into the sunshine.

It was such a nice day, I decided to take a little walk. I wandered down to the end of the lot, to the Haunted House set, where Miracle's blockbuster movie *Biker Vixens From Hell* was shot. Like the Miracle roller coaster, the Haunted House looked as if it had been made from old popsicle sticks. The only thing that kept it from falling apart, I suspected, were termites holding hands.

I wandered up to the front porch and peered in the windows. I knew the house was an illusion, a false front with nothing behind it. Nevertheless, as I looked inside, I half expected to see candelabras and Persian rugs and old furniture shrouded with cobwebs. Of course, I didn't see any of that. All I saw were some scaffolds and beyond that, the hookers strutting their stuff on Santa Monica Boulevard.

I sat down in a rusted glider and tried to pretend I was on the porch of a Malibu beach house, gazing out at the ocean, the sea breezes whipping through my hair.

Which wasn't all that easy to do, considering I was looking out at a row of metal Porta Potties.

I was swinging back and forth on the glider, listening to the rhythmic creaking of the old springs, when I remembered my mother's offer to fix me up with Ernie Lindstrom, the guy who was either a fireman or recently fired. Gad. The last thing I needed was a fix-up from my mom.

My mother means well, but she has this uncanny knack for digging up the world's most inappropriate men. Like that guy from her chat room who turned out to be a prisoner. And the engineering student from Laos who, when I asked him what he thought of Prozac, said, "She'd be delicious in a stew."

Besides, I was a grown woman; I could get my own dates. Well, actually I couldn't, but that was beside the point. I simply didn't want to go out with another one of Mom's walking disaster areas. I'd have to write her a very stern e-mail telling her so.

I sat on the glider a few minutes more, watching the sun shine on the Porta Potties. Then suddenly a squirrel came skittering across the porch with a bagel in his mouth. A humungous sesame bagel. Almost as big as he was. And from where I sat, it looked pretty darn good. A lot better than my brown mystery-meat sandwich.

"Hey, little fella," I said. "Want to trade lunches?"

The squirrel froze in his tracks and stood perfectly still, hoping that he and his bagel would blend in with the scenery.

"You give me your bagel," I said, "and I'll give you this lovely brown sandwich."

With that, he blinked twice and shot up the drainpipe. Obviously this was a squirrel with a discerning palate.

"Hey, you!"

I looked up and saw a security guard out in the roadway, perched on a golf cart, the main means of transportation on most studio lots. He was a beefy guy who looked like he was poured into his uniform and forgot to say "when." One deep breath, and the buttons on his shirt were history.

"No sitting on studio sets!" he shouted.

I picked up my sandwiches and got down off the porch.

"You're not supposed to leave the tour," he said as I approached the cart.

"I'm not a tourist," I bristled. "I'm a writer."

"Yeah?" His eyes squinted in disbelief. "What show?"

"Muffy 'n Me."

"Oh." He grinned. "You mean *Blazing Mattresses.* That's what we call it down at the guard house."

Apparently news of the Vanessa/Quinn boinkfest had reached the security department.

"I heard they had to send the bedspread out to be cleaned."

"I'd better get back to the office," I said, afraid that any minute now one of his shirt buttons would pop off and poke my eye out.

"Need a ride?" He patted the seat next to him and shot me a lascivious grin, no doubt hoping that all the women on the *Muffy* set were as promiscuous as its star.

"No, thanks. I'll walk."

"Suit yourself," he said, and took off down the road.

I waited till he was out of sight, then started back to the Writers' Building. I hadn't gone very far when I saw some trailers lined up behind the *Muffy 'n Me* soundstage. As I got closer I could see these were the actors' trailers, their names printed on the doors.

I couldn't help noticing that Vanessa's trailer was right next to Quinn's. If they were going to have sex, I wondered, why couldn't they just stay in their trailers? Why did they have to risk exposure by doing it on the soundstage? Clearly, they must have been turned on by the thrill of making love in a public place.

Suddenly I heard a woman's voice coming from Quinn's trailer.

"How could you, Quinn? I thought we meant something to each other."

It sounded like Audrey, but I couldn't be sure.

And then I did something foolish, almost as foolish as making love in a public place. I tiptoed up the steps of the trailer and listened at the door.

"Lighten up, Audrey," Quinn was saying. "You know as well as I do that our affair wasn't going anywhere. You're a married woman, and I'm a married man. What did you think—that I was going to leave my wife and run off with you?"

Audrey's voice was thick with emotion when she said, "Yes, Quinn, I did."

Quinn laughed.

"And wind up a lapdog like Stan? Forget it, sweetie. Besides, you're not really my type. I like 'em younger and wilder."

Although I couldn't see Audrey, I could picture her, her thin lips clamped shut, her blue eyes icy with rage.

"You're off the show, Quinn. You're history. I'm going to have you fired."

"Oh, really?" Quinn said. "Just try. The network loves me. They'll never let me go."

"I'll get you off this show," Audrey hissed, "if it's the last thing I do."

And then I heard her coming toward the door. I leaped off the steps and ducked around the side of the trailer just as the door flew open. I crouched down, praying Audrey wouldn't see me as she passed by. My heart pounding, I squeezed my eyes shut, too terrified to face her if she should discover me. I stayed that way for a minute or two. When I finally forced myself to open my eyes, Audrey was nowhere in sight.

That was the good news. The bad news was that I was not alone. For the first time I realized there was someone else crouched down behind me. I turned and looked at my companion.

It was Stan.

All the color had drained from his face. Obviously, he'd heard everything. I waited for him to say something, to read me the riot act, to fire me.

But all he did was reach for his Evian bottle.

Chapter Eight

"**H**ow delightful to see you again, my dear," Wells Dumont said, taking my hand and bringing it to his lips for a moist kiss.

It was four o'clock, and we were down on stage waiting for what's known as the "run-through" of "Cinderella Muffy" to begin. On most sitcoms, the actors run through the script at the end of the day, so the writers can see what's working, and what needs to be fixed.

Of course, what with all the real-life drama in the air that day, everyone had pretty much forgotten about my script.

Everyone except Wells.

"What a charming script," he said. "As I was saying the other day, it brings to mind a production of *Love's Labours Lost* I once starred in, back in England. That was right after my successful run as *Macbeth* in London's West End. And right before I came to America to play the Scottish thane on Broadway."

How pathetic, I thought. From *Macbeth* to *Muffy*. Talk about your downhill career slides.

"Perhaps some day you'll allow me to show you my scrapbook."

"That sounds great," I said, smiling wanly.

What was it with me and older guys, anyway? First

Mr. Goldman, and now Wells. For some strange reason, old coots seemed to find me wildly attractive.

"If you'll excuse me," I said, "I think I'll go get some coffee."

Tongues were wagging at full speed as I made my way across the stage to the buffet table. The production staff stood in gossipy clumps, shooting covert glances at Vanessa and Quinn.

The happy couple were sitting side by side on the sofa in the living room set, Vanessa pushing back her cuticles and Quinn whispering sweet nothings in her ear. Every once in a while, Quinn would glance over at Audrey, as if defying her to stop him. Once again, Audrey had reverted to Ice Queen mode. Whatever emotions were roiling inside her were invisible to the naked eye.

Not so for Zach Levy-Taylor, who could barely contain his rage at the sight of Quinn sitting thigh to thigh with his beloved Vanessa. Zach stood at the edge of the set, grinding his teeth and clenching his fists.

I poured myself some coffee, then eyed the buffet table, hoping to find some sticky buns left over from the actors' breakfast. Alas, there were none. All that had survived from breakfast was a bowl of dusty apples. Which was a blessing, actually. I'd have a nice healthy apple, only a hundred calories, with nary a fat globule.

I was just about to reach for one when I saw Danny, the production assistant, walk by with a chocolate chip cookie as big as a frisbee.

"Hey, Danny," I said. "Where'd you get the cookie?"

"Vending machine," he said. "Backstage."

I could practically read the thought bubble over his head: *Whoa, Tubby. I wouldn't do that if I were you.*

I smiled lamely. "It's for Kandi."

"Uh-huh," he said, nodding as if he actually believed me.

Danny's thought bubble was right, of course. The last thing I needed was a chocolate chip cookie as big as a frisbee. Absolutely the last thing. For once, I'd show a little restraint. I'd have a lo-cal apple, and that would be that.

Yeah, right. The minute Danny was gone, I sprinted backstage, tripping over cables, looking for the damn vending machine. I finally found it tucked in a dark corner. And there, in slot number C6, were the frisbee-esque chocolate chip cookies.

I fed a dollar bill into the machine and it spat out my cookie. I was just reaching down to retrieve it when I heard, "Those are my favorite."

I looked up and saw Stan, smiling shyly. He put in his dollar and pressed C6.

There we were, two fellow noshers, sneaking backstage for our sugar fixes. For the second time that day, Stan and I had bumped into each other in places we were ashamed to be seen.

"Really, Stan. We've got to stop meeting like this."

Of course I didn't say that. I didn't say anything. It was Stan who did the talking.

"I don't know how much you overheard outside Quinn's trailer today," he said. "But if I were you, I'd forget I ever heard it."

He was still smiling, but it was a hard-around-the-edges smile that made me slightly uneasy. Was it my imagination, or was mild-mannered Stan Miller actually threatening me?

Then, as quickly as it had come, his menacing air disappeared. Stan was back in doofus mode. He ripped off the cellophane from his cookie and gobbled it eagerly.

"Know what's also good?" he said. "D4. Grandma's Brownies."

And with that, he went waddling back on stage, wiping cookie crumbs from his lips.

*   *   *

Back at the buffet table, Kandi was pouring herself some coffee.

"God, this is excruciating," she sighed, watching Quinn run his finger along Vanessa's downy cheekbone. "I don't know how I could have ever been in love with him."

"Want a bite of my cookie?" I asked, holding out my chocolate chip frisbee.

Kandi shook her head and waved it away.

"If I ever fall in love again," she said, "shoot me."

"No problem."

I thought about telling her what I'd overheard outside Quinn's trailer, but decided against it. The last thing Kandi needed was incontrovertible evidence that Quinn had been cheating on her with Audrey as well as Vanessa.

We spent the next few minutes at the buffet table, Kandi unable to keep her eyes off Quinn and me wondering just how long it would take the chocolate chip cookie to take up permanent residence in my thighs.

Then suddenly we heard Dale Burton's voice behind us, raised in anger. We turned and saw him at the stage door, shouting into his cell phone. "Just tell Bernie to call me back!" For once, he seemed to be on a legitimate call. "This is the third time I've called today. Where the hell is he?" He slammed the phone shut and then realized that we'd been watching him. "Agents," he shrugged, with a forced laugh. "They're impossible, huh?"

So his agent wasn't returning his calls. Not a good sign.

He smiled feebly and headed back to join the other actors on stage.

"Okay, everybody," Audrey called out. "Let's get started."

At last, the run-through was about to begin.

Vanessa put the bubble gum she was chewing under the coffee table, and the show got under way. I stood with Stan, Audrey, and Kandi, each of us making notes in our script, checking off the jokes that worked, and making X's where the jokes died. Later, we'd return to the Writers' Building and think up new jokes for the failed X's.

Everything was going smoothly until the scene where Zach comes to pick up Muffy for the prom.

I guess it was an unfortunate choice of words, given the circumstances.

In the script, Quinn hands Vanessa over to Zach and tells him: "Don't do anything I wouldn't do."

It wouldn't have been so bad, if he hadn't said it with a suggestive leer that reminded everybody of exactly what he *had* done with Vanessa on the pink chenille bedspread. It was all too much for poor, lovestruck Zach.

"I'll kill you!" he said, lunging at Quinn.

I don't know how Zach built up his rather impressive set of muscles, but this much I do know: it wasn't from boxing. He must have thrown five punches at Quinn, all of which Quinn easily deflected.

"Calm down, kid," Quinn said, grabbing Zach's arms and pinning them behind his back. Zach struggled in vain to get free. But Quinn held on tightly, laughing, which just infuriated Zach all the more.

"I really would like to kill you, you slimebag!" he shouted, his face red with rage.

"You'll have to get in line for that," Quinn said.

Truer words were never spoken.

Somehow the actors managed to stumble through the rest of the run-through. But by now the script was the last thing on anybody's mind. Which, Kandi insisted, was a good thing.

"It means they'll leave your jokes alone," she said.

And she was right. We barely made any changes to the script that night. Audrey, looking uncharacteristically harried, sent us home early. I asked Kandi if she wanted to come over for dinner, but she was headed off to an emergency session with her shrink, Dr. Ira Mellman. Kandi has been seeing Dr. Mellman once a week for as long as I can remember. By now, she's probably paid off his mortgage and put his kids through college.

Sometimes I think seeing a therapist might be nice, but I know what Dr. Mellman charges, and all I can afford from him is a get-well card. Besides, I figure whatever problems I've got, I can solve with Dear Abby and a nice hot soak in the tub.

So Kandi and I said good-bye, and I drove home, stopping off for my own emergency therapy—a Koo Koo Roo chicken take-out dinner, with extra mashed potatoes.

"Hi, honey, I'm home," I called out to Prozac as I walked in the front door. I found her napping on my brand-new Ann Taylor silk sweater. She opened her eyes and glared at me balefully, then began kneading my sweater with her claws.

"Prozac," I wailed, "what are you doing?"

Of course, I knew exactly what she was doing. Getting even with me for leaving her alone all day.

I issued her a stern warning. "That kind of behavior simply won't be tolerated, young lady."

Okay, so I didn't issue any stern warnings. What I said was, "Look what I brought for dinner, lovebug! Roast chicken and mashed potatoes and brownies for dessert!"

She sniffed at the take-out bag, then shot me a look that said, "Great. And what will you be having?"

She wasn't kidding. I'm lucky I got to eat my half.

I know, I know. I shouldn't feed her people food. I shouldn't cave in to her emotional blackmail. I should be strong and firm and blah blah blah. What can I say? I'm a pillar of tapioca. If they gave free mileage for guilt trips, I'd never pay air fare again.

Prozac and I were stretched out on the sofa, Prozac alternately licking her mashed potatoes and her privates. I was gnawing on a chicken wing and going through my mail, when I came across a manila envelope. I opened it and pulled out a sheaf of papers. It was Lance's sitcom idea.

"If The Shoe Fits"
A Treatment for a Half-Hour Pilot
By Lance Venable

Welcome to the wacky world of shoes, where bunions are funny and laughter's just an instep away . . .

Ouch. This was going to be painful.

If The Shoe Fits turned out to be an ensemble comedy set in the shoe department of a high-end department store, starring a handsome yet hilarious shoe salesman by the name of Vance, an overbearing manager, a daffy ingenue salesgirl, and Vance's pet parrot, Manolo Blahnik. The gimmick behind Lance's show was that every week there'd be a famous guest customer. Or as Lance put it, "It's *Love Boat* with arch supports!"

I won't bore you with the excruciating details. Let just say that *If The Shoe Fits* made *Muffy 'n Me* look like something by Eugene O'Neill.

"Oh, jeez," I moaned to Prozac, "what am I going to tell Lance when he asks me how I liked it?"

We were both about to find out, because just then there was a knock on the door.

"Jaine! It's me, Lance."

I thought of pretending I wasn't home, but surely he knew I was there. With his x-ray hearing, he'd have heard me rattling around the apartment. I thought of pretending I was in the tub, but if I'd been in the tub, he would have heard the water running. I thought of making a break for it and sneaking out the back door, which seemed like a pretty good plan, until I remembered I didn't have a back door.

Oh, well. There was no getting out of it.

"I'm coming," I called out.

I opened the door, a brittle smile plastered on my face.

"Hi," I managed to squeak. "Come on in."

"So?" Lance asked. "Did you read it?"

That's it! I'd tell him I hadn't read it!

"Looks like you did read it," he said, pointing to the pages scattered on my coffee table.

Damn. Why did I leave them out like that?

"Uh . . . yes," I admitted. "I read it."

"And? What did you think?"

This wasn't going to be easy, but I had to tell him the truth. I'd just tell him, in a gentle yet honest way, that it stunk worse than a month-old pair of Odor-Eaters, and that it had about as much chance of selling as one of Prozac's poops.

"Well, Lance, actually, I . . ."

"Yes?" he said, eager as a puppy waiting to be adopted at the pound.

"I loved it."

Oh, God. Did those words actually come out of my mouth?

"I knew you would!" he grinned. "So, what should I do with it now?"

Put it in a shredder, then burn the remains and bury them. At least six feet under.

"Can you show it to the head writers on your show?" he asked. "Maybe they can do something with it."

Are you crazy? I want to work for these people. I can't hand them this piece of caca.

"Sure. I'll be happy to."

Obviously a demented doppelgänger had gotten hold of my powers of speech.

"Thanks, Jaine. You're an angel."

He gripped me in a viselike hug, then floated back to his apartment on a cloud of unrealistic expectations.

"What the hell is wrong with me?" I asked Prozac when he was gone.

She shot me a look that said, *Don't get me started.*

And then I realized: There was an easy way out. I'd simply hold on to the treatment for a few weeks and pretend that Audrey had read it and turned it down. This way I'd let Audrey be the bad guy. A role I suspected she was eminently suited for.

I tossed the skeletal remains of our chicken dinner into the trash, then headed for the bathtub, where I soaked for a good forty-five minutes. There's nothing quite so relaxing as a hot soak, especially if it's accompanied by a cool chardonnay.

And I needed all the relaxation I could get. Tomorrow was Friday, tape day, the day my script would be recorded for posterity. Who knew? Maybe *Muffy 'n Me* would run long enough to go into syndication. Maybe decades (even centuries!) from now, generations of slack-jawed insomniacs would be watching my show in re-runs on Nick at Nite. This could be my ticket to immortality.

I only hoped we could make it through the taping without a fistfight.

YOU'VE GOT MAIL!

TO: Shoptillyoudrop
FROM: Jausten
SUBJECT: Do NOT give my number to Ernie
Lindstrom!

Do NOT give my number to Ernie Lindstrom!
Do NOT give my number to Ernie Lindstrom!
Do NOT give my number to Ernie Lindstrom!

TO: Jausten
FROM: Shoptillyoudrop
SUBJECT: Flipped Out

All right, dear. You've made your point. I won't give
your number to Ernie Lindstrom, even though Edna
has been positively begging me to.

Like I said in my last e-mail, your father has
completely flipped out. This morning he was standing
at the bathroom mirror counting the hairs in his ears.
What sort of man goes around counting his ear hairs?
"Oh, God," he kept saying, "I've got more hair in my
ears than on my head."

And yesterday I caught him snooping in my car. He
pretended he was looking for a Kleenex! We have
boxes and boxes of Price Club Kleenex in the linen
closet, and he expects me to believe he's looking for a
Kleenex in my Camry. There's no doubt about it. Your
daddy needs psychiatric help. I'm seriously thinking
about slipping some antidepressants into his
Wheatena, but how would I get my hands on antidepressants? I don't suppose you could run down to

Mexico and pick up some for me, could you, darling?
If not, I'll order some St. John's Wort from Home
Shopping, only $39.95, plus shipping and handling.

That's all for now. Got to run to the dentist.

Mom

TO: Jausten
FROM: Daddyo
SUBJECT: Exhibit "A"

I have proof positive that your mother is having an affair. Yesterday I happened to be looking for a Kleenex
in her car, when I found a bottle of Love Oil!

TO: Daddyo
FROM: Jausten
SUBJECT: Huh?

Love oil? What do you mean? Love oil?

TO: Jausten
FROM: Daddyo
SUBJECT: Wake up and Smell the Coffee, Part II

You know. The stuff they advertise in the back of
men's magazines. Right next to the inflatable sex
dolls. Your mom and Mr. Koskovalis probably rub it
on each other, as a prelude to their sick, kinky sex.

TO: Jausten
FROM: Shoptillyoudrop
SUBJECT: Love Oil

Wait till you hear the latest. Your father claims he
found a bottle of "love oil" in my Camry. I asked him
to show it to me. He went out to the car, and searched
high and low, but of course he didn't find any "love
oil" because there was no love oil to find. I really
think he should be seeing a therapist. Please ask
Kelsey Grammer if he knows a good one here in
Florida.

TO: Shoptillyoudrop
FROM: Jausten

Mom, Kelsey Grammer isn't really a therapist. He just
plays one on TV.

TO: Jausten
FROM: Shoptillyoudrop

How about his brother Niles? Maybe you could ask
him.

Chapter Nine

"For this, I'm missing Jeopardy?"

Mr. Goldman was pissed. He and the rest of the Shalom gang were in the audience waiting for the taping of my show to begin. They'd been sitting there, cooling their heels, for the past forty-five minutes. The show was supposed to have started taping at seven, but we had to wait for Stan and Audrey to get back from a network meeting out in Burbank. According to Bianca, they were stuck in a massive traffic jam on the Hollywood Freeway.

I'd come out into the audience to say hello to my students and was beginning to wish I hadn't.

The young comic who'd been hired to keep the audience in a festive, ready-to-laugh-at-anything mood (known in sitcom circles as the warm-up guy) was getting desperate. He'd long since run through his supply of jokes and was now asking the audience to hum the theme songs from their favorite sitcoms.

"Feh," Mr. Goldman said in a stage whisper that could be heard in Pomona. "You call that funny? That's not funny."

Unfortunately, the rest of the audience seemed to agree with him. People were squirming in their seats and looking at their watches. Great. Just what I needed. An audience of malcontents.

"I'm hungry," Mr. Goldman whined. "They keep us waiting so long, they should serve refreshments. A canapé. A pig in a blanket. A potato puff, maybe."

"Have a Tic Tac," Mrs. Pechter said.

"I don't like Tic Tacs. I like Certs."

Mrs. Pechter rolled her eyes in annoyance.

"And where's Vanessa?" Goldman said. "I didn't come all the way across town to see some pisher comic. I came to see the babe with the big tits."

"Please, Mr. Goldman. There are youngsters in the audience."

"Okay, I came to see the babe with the big bazooms. Is that better?"

"You're impossible, Abe," Mrs. Pechter said, shooting me a sympathetic look.

"You think maybe you could get me Vanessa's autograph?" Mr. Goldman asked.

"Sure," I said, eager to escape. "I'll see if I can find her."

"See if you can find some food, too," he shouted after me. "An M&M would be nice."

I hurried backstage, where I found Wells and Zach hanging out at the coffee machine. Wells was telling Zach about the time he played Mercutio to Laurence Olivier's Romeo. Zach was pretending to give a damn.

"Hi," I said. "Sorry to interrupt, but have either of you seen Vanessa?"

"No," Zach grunted, clearly upset at having been reminded of his lost love.

"I believe she and Quinn are still in their dressing rooms," Wells said.

Zach clenched his fists into angry balls. No doubt he was thinking what I was thinking: that Vanessa and Quinn were probably together in the same dressing room, boinking their brains out.

Out on stage, the warm-up guy was scraping the bottom of the comedy barrel and doing knock-knock jokes.

"Knock knock. Who's there? Aardvark. Aardvark who? Aardvark a million miles for one of your smiles!"

The audience groaned.

"Oh, God," I said. "They're in such a bad mood. If this keeps up, I'll be lucky if they don't lynch me."

"Don't worry, my dear," Wells said. "I'll entertain them."

And before I could stop him, he went bounding out onto the stage.

I watched in the wings as he walked up to the warm-up guy and whispered something in his ear.

"And now, ladies and gentlemen," the comic said, "as a special treat, allow me to present Mr. Wells Dumont doing Hamlet's soliloquy from the blockbuster hit, *Hamlet!*"

The audience gave a tepid round of applause as Wells tried his best to look like a twenty-something Danish prince.

"To be or not to be . . ." he began.

What on earth did he think he was doing? These people came to see a comedy. Not a guy contemplating suicide. Even knock-knock jokes were better than Hamlet's bitching and moaning.

As Wells rambled on, the natives grew more and more restless. People were openly yawning; I saw a guy in the third row nodding off. Clearly, I could kiss my show biz career good-bye. Woody Allen sitting on Neil Simon's lap couldn't get laughs from this crowd.

It was all too painful to watch, so I made my way out a side door into the cool night air. I sat down on the steps of the soundstage, looking up at what would have been the stars if the smog hadn't been so thick. I could barely make out the Miracle roller coaster in the distance.

But one thing I could see was Dale, a few feet away, talking on his cell phone. At first I couldn't hear what he was saying, but then suddenly he started shouting.

"If you won't do something about it, I will!" He punched the air with his fist to emphasize his point. "That's right, Bernie. I'll handle it myself."

With that, he snapped his phone shut and stormed past me back into the soundstage. No hello. No hint of recognition. As if he hadn't even seen me.

And what was that phone call all about? Just what was Dale Burton going to handle?

Whatever it was, I didn't much care. I had troubles enough of my own. Not only was my career about to go up in flames, but there was a distinct possibility that my father was losing his marbles. What was all that non-sense about finding love oil in Mom's car? Of course, it was possible that he wasn't nuts and that Mom was actually having an affair with some sleazeball from the shopping channel, but that thought was just too horrible to contemplate.

So there I sat, whiling away the minutes, feeling my fanny go numb and thinking about joining a nunnery to get away from it all, when Kandi came rushing up.

"Where the hell have you been?" I asked.

"Emergency shrink session."

"Didn't you just have one of those yesterday?"

"Hey, I'm having a rough time."

"Join the party," I said.

"How come you're out here? Why aren't you inside?"

"The taping hasn't started yet. Stan and Audrey are stuck on the Hollywood Freeway."

"I was, too," she said. "It's a nightmare out there."

"It couldn't have been worse than what's going on in there," I said, pointing to the stage.

"Why? What happened?"

"The warm-up guy ran out of jokes forty minutes

ago, and when last I looked, Wells was entertaining the troops with Hamlet's soliloquy."

"You poor thing." Kandi shook her head pityingly. "We'd better get in there before Stan and Audrey show up."

With Herculean strength, she managed to haul me up and drag me back inside. By now, Wells was back at the coffee machine, telling poor trapped Zach about the time he played Iago to Paul Robeson's Othello.

"Jaine, my dear," he said, catching sight of me, "I tried to warm them up for you. Although I must admit, they weren't the most responsive audience I've ever played to."

"Of course, they weren't responsive. Do you really think people who come to a taping of *Muffy 'n Me* are Shakespeare fans?"

Okay, so I didn't really say that. What I said was: "Thanks for trying."

Kandi and I left Wells and Zach at the coffee machine and made our way out to the audience, where, to my horror, I saw the warm-up guy handing his microphone to Mr. Goldman. The nunnery was looking better every minute.

"You think you're so funny?" the warm-up guy said. "You take over."

"Okay, sonny. I will!"

Mr. Goldman grabbed the mike and cleared his throat, a phlegmy affair that nauseated everyone. But before he could say anything, Audrey came marching onto the set, Stan huffing behind her. Kandi and I hurried over to join them.

"Let's get this show on the road," Audrey said.

"But I'm not finished," Mr. Goldman protested, refusing to let go of the mike.

Audrey looked over and saw Mr. Goldman in the section reserved for guests of the cast and crew.

"Who invited that idiot?" she whispered, looking around accusingly.

"That would be me," I admitted. "He's one of my students from the Shalom Retirement Home."

I smiled weakly, wondering if they'd let me bring my vibrator to the nunnery.

Mr. Goldman cleared his throat again, sounding a lot like a clogged toilet.

"Knock knock," he said defiantly. "Who's there? Fornication. Fornication who? Fornication like this, you should wear a black tie."

Believe it or not, he got a laugh. Probably the last I'd be hearing all night.

Chapter Ten

It turned out I was wrong about the laughs. After the first few apathetic minutes, the audience stopped coughing and started laughing.

Cancel the nunnery. Call the movers. It looked like I'd be moving to Malibu after all.

The first scene featured Wells as Mr. Watkins the nosy neighbor and Quinn as Uncle Biff. Mr. Watkins stops by, convinced that Muffy has turned his cat into an umbrella stand. The script called for Uncle Biff to offer Mr. Watkins a donut. Mr. Watkins refuses, and Uncle Biff eats it himself.

That was what was supposed to happen.

"Won't you join me in a box of donuts?" Quinn was supposed to say, holding out the box.

Then Wells was supposed to say, "I doubt there's room in there for both of us."

Then the audience was supposed to laugh uproariously.

None of which happened.

Because when Quinn went to the kitchen counter for the donuts, he came back empty-handed.

"Sorry," he said, abandoning the script. "There aren't any donuts."

"Props!" Audrey shouted, fuming. "Where the hell are the donuts?"

We all looked around for Marco, the prop guy, but he was nowhere to be seen.

Then Teri, the makeup lady, stepped forward, none too thrilled at the prospect of facing an angry Audrey.

"Marco had to go to the hospital," she stammered. "His wife was about to give birth. I was supposed to tell you, but I forgot. You see, I ran out of mascara, and I had to run over to the drugstore to get some, and I guess it just slipped my mind."

The poor woman was so scared, she was practically peeing in her pants.

Audrey smiled wearily.

"That's okay, honey," she said. "No problem."

Teri breathed a sigh of relief and skittered back to the makeup room.

The minute she was gone, Audrey turned to Stan and hissed, "Fire her."

"Will somebody please go to the prop room and get the damn donuts?" the director shouted from the control booth.

"I'll go," Kandi said.

As she hurried off, Mr. Goldman called after her: "Bring one for me, too, sweetie! A person could die of starvation around here."

Which got another big laugh from the audience. Mr. Goldman grinned proudly. Maybe he was as funny as Seinfeld, after all.

Minutes later, Kandi returned with the donuts.

"Okay," the director called out. "Let's take it from the top."

So once again, Mr. Watkins showed up, convinced that Muffy had turned his cat into an umbrella stand. Once again, Uncle Biff tried unsuccessfully to mollify him with a donut.

Only this time there was a pastry box on the counter. Quinn brought it back to the table.

"Sure you won't have one?"

He held out the box to Mr. Watkins, but Watkins waved it away.

"You'll be sorry," Quinn said, plucking a sugar-coated donut from the box. But as it turned out, Quinn was the sorry one. He took one mouthful and grimaced.

"I think there's something wrong with this do—"

But before he could utter his last "nut," he doubled over in pain, his face a nasty shade of blue.

Wells raced to his side.

"Good heavens," he said, horrified, as Quinn crumpled to the floor. "I think he's dead."

From the audience, I could hear Mr. Goldman: "That's funny? A guy dying is supposed to be funny? I don't get it."

"Shut up, Abe," Mrs. Pechter said. "I think the poor man is really dead."

"Oy vey."

My sentiments exactly.

Chapter
Eleven

Ever notice how, when your apartment gets burglarized, you could reach menopause waiting for the cops to show up? But have a TV star die on a soundstage, and they're on the scene faster than calories cling to my hips.

The cops showed up in record time that night. Before I knew it, they'd cordoned off the kitchen set with yellow police tape and were questioning the cast and crew. I assured the cop who questioned me that I'd seen or heard nothing suspicious that evening.

By now, the audience was buzzing. Now *this* was entertainment. This was something they could tell the folks about back home.

I hurried over to make sure my students were okay. I didn't want one of them keeling over with a heart attack from all the excitement.

"Is he really dead?" Mrs. Rubin asked.

"Given the fact that he hasn't been breathing for the past twenty minutes, I'd say yes."

"Such a tragedy," she tsk-tsked.

"You think it was a heart attack?" Mrs. Pechter asked.

"Of course not," Mr. Goldman hummphed. "The guy was poisoned. Anybody could see that."

"I'll never eat donuts again," said Mrs. Rubin.

"You shouldn't be eating them anyway," said Mrs. Pechter. "Not with your high cholesterol."

"Her cholesterol isn't as high as my cholesterol," Mr. Goldman boasted. "Nobody has high cholesterol like I do."

And so it went, until the cops decided to let the audience go. Reluctantly, they filed out of their seats, giving their names to the police as they left the building. The last thing I heard Mr. Goldman say as they ushered him out the door was, "I still say they could've served refreshments."

At which point, Kandi came rushing up to me.

"Guess what," she said. "The cops think the sugar on the donut wasn't sugar. They think it was poison. Probably rat poison."

I looked over at poor Quinn, slumped over at the kitchen table. The guy was a rat, but he certainly didn't deserve to die like one.

"What if they think I did it?" Kandi raked her fingers through her hair distractedly.

"Don't be silly. Why would they think that?"

"I was the one who brought him the donuts, wasn't I?"

"Kandi, you're overreacting. Never in a million years are they going to think you had anything to do with Quinn's murder."

"Excuse me, Ms. Tobolowski?"

We turned to see a dark-haired young cop standing at our side.

"Yes," Kandi said, "I'm Kandi Tobolowski."

"Would you mind coming down to the precinct with us? We'd like to ask you a few questions."

"I didn't do it," Kandi wailed, like a suspect trapped in a Perry Mason episode. "I swear, I didn't do it!"

"Nobody said you did anything, Ms. Tobolowski," the cop said. "We just want to ask you a few questions."

"I want my lawyer."

"Okay, fine. Call your lawyer."

Then it dawned on her:

"Oh, gee. I don't have a lawyer."

"What about that guy who got you a settlement when you hurt yourself on that defective stairmaster?" I asked.

"Oh, right. Ramon Sandoval. Call him and tell him to meet me down at police headquarters."

"What's his phone number?"

"1-800-WE SUE 4 U."

Uh-oh. Not exactly F. Lee Bailey, was he?

"Tell his answering service it's urgent."

"Don't worry," I said. "I'll take care of it."

I walked Kandi out to the squad car, where we were horrified to see a bunch of news vans in the parking lot. Suddenly reporters were swooping down on us like flies on a Belgian waffle.

Kandi covered her face and ducked into the car.

"I'll never work again," she moaned.

"Don't worry, honey. Everything's going to be fine," I assured her with a confidence I didn't feel. "As soon as I call Sandoval, I'll drive over to the police station and wait for you."

Which is exactly what I did.

It wasn't till I was pulling up in front of the Hollywood Precinct that I remembered Dale and his angry phone call. I'd told the cop who questioned me that I'd seen nothing suspicious. But now I remembered the look of grim determination on Dale's face as he spoke to his agent.

"If you won't do something about it," he'd said, "I will."

Maybe the "it" he was talking about was Quinn taking over his role in *Muffy 'n Me*. And maybe the "something" Dale threatened to do was knock off his competition with a dose of rat poison.

* * *

I spent the next four hours waiting for Kandi in the lobby of the Hollywood Precinct. Not exactly a ride in the wine country. Although they did have more than their fair share of winos stumbling around.

I sat next to a tall guy in a baby-blue sharkskin suit and enough gold chains around his neck to stock the jewelry department at the Home Shopping Club. This is just a wild stab in the dark, but I think he might have been a pimp.

All I know is, he offered me a job.

"Some of my clients," he told me with a wink, "they like 'em hefty."

I assured him I was gainfully employed and had no need of his services.

"You ever change your mind, honey, you just call Leon." And with that, he handed me his business card. *Leon's Escort Service. Let us Escort you to Ecstasy.*

I have to admit I was a tad relieved when three of Leon's employees were released from custody, and Leon finally left. I spent the rest of the time trying not to stare at the flamboyant same-sex couple sitting across from me. Exactly which sex they were, I'm still trying to figure out.

After what seemed like an eternity, Kandi finally emerged from captivity, with a handsome Latino guy by her side. This was her attorney, Ramon Sandoval, Mr. WE SUE 4 U.

"Don't worry, Kandi," he assured her. "they've got nothing on you."

"But what if they arrest me?"

"I hope they do."

"What?"

"We'll sue them for wrongful imprisonment!"

And before you could say "ambulance chaser," Ramon was out the door. Kandi and I followed him out to the parking lot. Luckily there were no reporters waiting to ambush us. I insisted that Kandi spend the night with me; I didn't want her to be alone.

"Thanks, Jaine," she smiled gratefully. "I really could use the company."

We drove back to my place, making a pit stop at the supermarket to pick up several emergency pints of Ben & Jerry's Chunky Monkey ice cream. A half hour later we were cuddled in bed, inhaling our Chunky Monkeys, Prozac licking the lids.

When we'd scraped every last molecule from the cartons, Kandi put down her spoon with a sigh.

"It was rat poison, all right. The cops had the donuts tested. And they think I'm the one who did it."

"But why? Anyone could have slipped into the prop room and doctored those donuts."

"Yes, but I'm the one who brought them to Quinn."

"But if you were really the murderer, you wouldn't have brought him the donuts. If you knew they were poisoned, the last thing you'd do would be to implicate yourself that way. Surely, the cops will figure that out."

"There's something else," she said with a sigh.

"What?"

"Bianca told them what I said the other day."

"What did you say the other day?" I asked, totally befuddled.

"Remember when Bianca stopped by our office to drop off those scripts? I guess I was saying something about wanting to kill Quinn."

"Oh, geez. That's right. You did."

"You've got to help me, Jaine. You've got to find the killer. Just like you did last year."

(It's true. I solved a murder last year; it's a long story, one you can read all about in *This Pen for Hire*, now available in paperback at a bookstore near you.)

"Until the real killer is found," Kandi said, "I'm the

one everyone will associate with the crime. I'm the one the cops hauled off for questioning."

"Of course, I'll do what I can. But I'm just an amateur."

"Yeah," said Kandi, "but you're an amateur who cares about me."

That I was.

We woke up the next morning like two drunks on a bender, our faces still sticky from Chunky Monkey ice cream. We turned on the TV, just in time to see news footage of Kandi being hauled off in the squad car.

"Oh, wow," she moaned. "I look so fat."

Don't you just hate it when Size Sixes say they look fat?

"Kandi, get your priorities straight. We've got more important things to worry about than how you look on television."

"Look," she said. "There's a shot of you, waving good-bye to me."

"Yikes! Look at my tush! It's taking up half the screen."

What can I say? Sometimes it's tough to prioritize.

"I'm going on a diet," Kandi announced.

"Me, too."

"I'm going to start right after I finish this," she said, lifting a sticky bun from the box of pastry I'd picked up last night at the market.

"Me, too," I said, grabbing one.

Prozac passed up a sticky bun for a bowl of fish guts. Which is why you'll never find a cat editing *Gourmet* magazine.

"What you need," I said to Kandi after we'd polished off our breakfast, "is a nice relaxing weekend. Maybe we'll drive out to the beach, have some margaritas in

Malibu, then come home and watch old movies while we stuff ourselves with pizza."

"What about our diet?"

"We'll start Monday."

"Sounds like a plan." She managed a small smile. "I don't know what I'd do without you, Jaine."

She took my hand and squeezed it. I squeezed back.

Sad, but true: I experienced more intimacy in that three-second hand squeeze with Kandi than I did in three years of marriage to The Blob.

Kandi tootled off to the shower, and I was busy cleaning up the breakfast things, when the phone rang.

It was Bianca. I felt like slapping her silly for getting Kandi in trouble with the cops.

"What the hell do you want, you sniveling little ratfink?"

Okay, what I really said was: "Hello, Bianca."

"Audrey asked me to call you. She wants you and Kandi to come to the studio today for an emergency rewrite session, to write Quinn out of the script."

Good heavens. The body was barely cold. They sure weren't wasting any time, were they?

"She wants us to come in on a Saturday?"

"And Sunday, too."

So much for our relaxing weekend.

"Lots of sitcom writers work weekends, Jaine," she said reprovingly. "It comes with the territory. By the way, do you know where Kandi is? I've been trying to reach her all morning."

"She's here with me."

"Oh." Did I detect a note of disappointment in her voice? Was she expecting Kandi to be in jail? "Then you can tell her about the rewrites."

She hung up without bothering to say good-bye.

What a bitch. I wouldn't mind seeing her in jail. If only she was the murderer. And then it occurred to me: Maybe she *was*. What if Bianca, like Audrey and Kandi, had been boffing Quinn? True, it was hard to conceive of anyone wanting to sleep with a creep like Bianca, but there's no accounting for tastes. Maybe Quinn had a thing for girls with ferrety faces. What if they'd been sleeping together, and when Bianca found out about his affair with Vanessa, she blew a gasket? Was it possible that she was the one who'd sprinkled rat poison on the donut and then pointed the finger of suspicion at Kandi?

Hey, this was Hollywood. Where anything was possible. And everyone seemed to have been sleeping with Quinn Kirkland.

Chapter
Twelve

Instead of margaritas in Malibu, we went through re-write hell in Hollywood. Killing off Quinn on paper was a lot tougher than it had been in real life. Whenever we could, we gave his lines to Dale. But it wasn't easy. I sat by, helpless, as some of my best jokes were cut from the script. I was beginning to understand why comedy writers often wind up in the Home for the Terminally Frustrated.

The rewrite was no picnic for Kandi, either. I could tell her mind was a million miles away. I'd be distracted, too, faced with the prospect—however remote—of spending the rest of my life in an unflattering prison jumpsuit.

Audrey was surprisingly sympathetic.

"I know you're upset, Kandi," she said. "But I want you to know that I don't believe for a minute that you had anything to do with this crime."

Kandi smiled gratefully.

Now you know Kandi didn't kill Quinn. And I knew Kandi didn't kill Quinn. But I couldn't help wondering: Why was Audrey so sure Kandi didn't kill Quinn? Was it because she did it herself? I remembered the rage in her voice when she confronted Quinn in his dressing room. Was it possible she'd made a pit stop in the prop room on her way back from her network meeting?

Just something to think about between paragraphs.

Monday morning we gathered on stage for another read-through of *Cinderella Muffy*. Had it been only a week since I first showed up at the studio? It felt like months.

Audrey made a perfunctory speech about how everyone was going to miss Quinn, what a fine actor he was, what a credit to the show, blah blah blah. But it was clear she didn't mean a word of it. She spoke in a dull monotone, a Stepford Wife dressed in Armani.

As she spoke, everyone sat around the long metal table, eyes lowered, nodding their heads in agreement. Everyone except Stan, who stared straight ahead, guzzling his gin at an alarming rate.

Dale made a pathetic attempt to look subdued, but you didn't have to be Sigmund Freud to figure out he was overjoyed. Every once in a while, he'd break out in a wide grin, thrilled with all his new lines. For once, his cell phone was nowhere in sight.

Zach, too, was in Happy Camper mode. He sat by Vanessa's side, fetching her coffee and danish, like one of the Tarleton twins at Tara, glad to be back in her orbit.

As for Vanessa, she sat woodenly throughout the reading, her emotions locked away somewhere deep inside her. She gave no clue as to what she was thinking. It could have been, *I can't go on living without my beloved Quinn.*

Or, *I need a pedicure.*

Your guess is as good as mine.

Of all the actors, only Wells seemed genuinely saddened by Quinn's demise.

"Poor Quinn," he said, shaking his head sadly. "What a talented fellow he was. I still can't believe he's gone."

But I had to remind myself: Wells was an actor. For all I knew, he could have been in the middle of a very convincing performance.

After a suitable period of mostly manufactured grief, the actors started reading the script. Dale delivered his new lines with gusto, really selling the jokes. He wasn't as funny as Quinn, but he wasn't bad. Not bad at all. I think everyone was surprised at how many laughs he was getting.

Audrey and Stan exchanged glances, clearly impressed with his performance.

We were almost through with the reading when I noticed a short, pudgy guy walking onto the set. He looked bewildered, like a tourist who'd wandered off from his tram.

"Can I help you?" Audrey asked, not sounding the least bit helpful.

"I'm Detective Incorvia," the man said. "L.A.P.D."

"Omigosh," Kandi whispered, squeezing my elbow. "That's the cop who questioned me the other night."

He rummaged around in his pocket and finally came up with a badge.

Audrey stared at it for a second or two. Then, apparently convinced that it didn't come from a Cracker Jacks box, she smiled stiffly.

"What can I do for you, Detective?"

Was it my imagination, or did she seem a tad nervous?

"I need to ask you and your staff a few questions. Is there somewhere I can conduct my interviews?"

"Oh. Of course. You can use the conference room in the Writers' Building."

He took out a beat-up notepad from his pocket and consulted it.

"The first person I'd like to talk to is . . ."

He squinted down at the paper, trying to decipher his own handwriting.

". . . Jaine Austen."

Everyone was staring at me. Now I knew how Kandi felt the other night. My palms starting gushing sweat. I smiled weakly at Detective Incorvia. He didn't smile back.

Damn. What if I'd just taken Kandi's place as the cops' Number One Suspect?

Chapter
Thirteen

Detective Incorvia was a harmless-looking guy, with soft brown eyes and a fuzzy mustache that badly needed trimming. So why was I so damn nervous? I sat across from him in the conference room, my palms still gushing like Niagara. I told myself I was being crazy. He said he wanted to talk to everybody, not just me. This was strictly routine. But all I could think about was me, in Kandi's unflattering prison jumpsuit, sharing a cell with a gal named Duke.

Incorvia reached down into a paper bag on the floor beside him and pulled out a stethoscope.

"Ever seen this before?" he asked.

It was the stethoscope Kandi had swiped from the prop room.

"We found it in your friend's desk," he said.

"Oh?" I tried to feign innocence.

"It's been missing from the prop room for the past two months. We believe Ms. Tobolowski stole it."

"She didn't steal it. She just borrowed it."

"Steal. Borrow. Whatever you want to call it. Your friend obviously likes to hang out in the prop room."

"Look, Detective," I said with as much authority as I could muster. "Kandi didn't kill Quinn. She simply couldn't have done it."

"Apparently she was having an affair with him."

"So were half the women in greater Los Angeles."

"And she was overheard threatening to kill him."

"That's not true! She didn't threaten to kill him. She just said she'd *like to* kill him. It was all very hypothetical, like me saying I'd like to lose twenty pounds by the weekend."

"I stand corrected," he said, a smile hovering on his lips.

"And she wasn't the only one who was angry at Quinn," I went on.

"Oh?"

I told him about Zach and how he'd attacked Quinn during rehearsal. About Dale's angry phone call to his agent. And about Audrey's confrontation with Quinn in his trailer, how she threatened to get rid of him if it was the last thing she did.

He took out a well-chewed pencil and made notes as I talked.

"I'm telling you, lots of people were pissed at Quinn. The man had more enemies than Nixon. Anyone could have slipped into the prop room while Marco was gone and doctored that donut."

"Not anyone," Incorvia said. "During the forty-five minutes the prop room was left unattended, the director was up in the control booth with his assistant director. The cameramen were backstage playing poker. And Bianca, the Millers' secretary, was with Danny the production assistant."

Damn. Bianca had an alibi.

"And the old guy. Wells Dumont. He was with Zach Levy-Taylor the whole time—except when he was on stage doing his soliloquy from *Hamlet*."

So Wells had an alibi, too. I was glad to hear it. It looked as though his grief had been genuine, after all.

"What about Quinn's wife?"

"She lives in New York."

"So? She could've flown out here, shown up at the studio disguised as a tourist, poisoned the donuts, and then flown back again."

Incorvia shot me a skeptical look. Even I wasn't buying that theory.

"At the time of the murder, Quinn's wife was at Elaine's restaurant in New York City, having drinks with Regis and Joy Philbin."

"That still leaves a lot people who could have done it," I insisted.

Incorvia nodded. "Including yourself."

Oh, crud. I was back in that damn prison jumpsuit again.

"Relax," he said. "I asked around about you, Ms. Austen. I know you helped solve a murder in Westwood last year. So I'm reasonably certain you had nothing to do with this crime."

"What about Kandi?" I asked. "You don't really think she did it, do you?"

"Her, I'm not so sure about."

"You've got to believe me. My best friend is simply not a murderer."

"That's what Ted Bundy's best friend said."

He flipped the pages in his notebook until he came to a clean page.

"One final question before you go," he said.

"Yes?"

He leaned forward in his chair.

"What's the best way to get an agent?"

Huh???

"You see, I'm writing this screenplay, about a cop in Hollywood. . . ."

I couldn't believe it. Kandi was right. Everyone in L.A. has a script to sell. I wouldn't be surprised to come home one of these days and find Prozac banging one out on my computer.

"It's a zany action-comedy-thriller," he said. "Alfred Hitchcock meets Jackie Chan."

Holy Moses. First Lance, now this.

"Actually, I don't have an agent," I demurred.

"Too bad," he sighed. "Oh, well. Maybe you'd like to read it when I'm through. Give me some notes."

The last thing I wanted to witness was Alfred Hitchcock meeting Jackie Chan. The guy was nuts if he thought I'd waste my time reading his stupid script.

"Sure," I said, smiling brightly. "I'd love to."

Back in our office, Kandi was lying on the sofa, staring at the ceiling, a copy of *Variety* spread open across her chest like a funeral shroud.

"The worst has happened," she moaned.

"What's wrong?"

She pointed to the *Variety*. I read the headline: *Cops Quiz Comedy Scribe*.

"I always wanted to make the front page of *Variety*. But not like this. I'll never work again."

"Of course you will. Everyone's going to forget all about this."

"Right. Just like they forgot about O.J. Simpson."

"Don't be silly," I said. "By next week, this'll be old news."

I smiled brightly, but Kandi just lay there like a poster child for Clinical Depression.

"By the way," she said, "my agent dumped me today."

"Oh, no."

"She said she was on 'client overload,' and it wasn't fair to keep me on since she was no longer able to give me the attention I deserved. And so she's turning me over to a hot new agent in the office."

"A hot new agent? That sounds great."

"The 'hot new agent' is a kid in the mail room. The guy has zero clout. Even his own mother doesn't return his phone calls."

She took the *Variety* and put it over her face.

"Come on, honey," I said. "As soon as they catch the real killer, you'll be in the clear, and agents will be lining up to represent you."

"As soon as *you* catch the real killer." She peeked out from under the *Variety*, and looked at me pleadingly. "Really, Jaine. I'm counting on you to get me out of this mess."

Oh, great. There wasn't *too* much pressure on me, was there?

"I'll do all I can," I promised. "But you mustn't give up on the police. Detective Incorvia seemed like a very capable guy."

"But he thinks I did it," she said, tossing the *Variety* in the trash.

"No, he doesn't," I fibbed. "He's got lots of suspects he's investigating."

"Yeah, but why do I get the feeling I'm leading the pack?"

"That's not true," I fibbed again.

"Why? What did he say at your meeting?"

I gave her a carefully edited version of our meeting, leaving out the part about the stethoscope and Ted Bundy's best friend.

"Honestly, Kandi," I said. "Incorvia seems like a nice guy. I seriously doubt he has an agenda to see you in jail."

She sat up, somewhat relieved.

"How about we go grab some lunch?" I asked.

"No, I can't face anybody right now."

"Okay, I'll go to the commissary and get us something. What do you want?"

"Hemlock on rye," she sighed. "And if they're all out of that, get me Today's Special. It's probably just as lethal."

She smiled wanly.

I was happy to see she still had a sense of humor. It looked like she was going to need it.

I stood at the steam table, watching Helga dish out two portions of thick white glop into Styrofoam take-out containers. According to Helga, it was tuna noodle casserole. It looked a lot more like wet plaster to me.

Really, I decided, it was much too vile to eat. It's one thing to get fat on Sara Lee, another thing to pork up on plaster. Besides, weren't Kandi and I supposed to be on diets?

I'd just have to change my order. I looked at Helga, at her Brillo hair, her pencil-thin lips, and the hairy wart on her receding chin. God, she was scary. Maybe I should just pay for it and toss it in the dumpster outside. No. No way. I really had to develop some backbone if I intended to keep doing this detective stuff.

I took a deep breath and shored up my courage. So what if she got angry? What's the worst she could do? Hit me with her hair net?

"I hate to be a bother," I said, "but is it to late to change my order?"

She glared at me, the same look she probably gave to her subordinates in the Gestapo. Then she dumped the gloppy white stuff back into the serving tray.

"Whaddaya want?" she grunted.

"Do you have any salads?"

"We got egg salad and potato salad."

"Don't you have anything green?"

"Just the mold on the egg salad."

I wound up driving to McDonald's for two Shake-a-

Salads. It was so much nicer being waited on by a sullen teenager than a sullen ex-Nazi.

I was just making my way back onto the lot, when I saw Wells Dumont pull up behind me in an elegant old Mercedes.

"I see the commissary food is beginning to get to you," he said, when we got out of our cars. He eyed my McDonald's take-out bag. "Quinn used to say that flies came to the commissary to commit suicide."

I laughed. It was an old joke (Henny Youngman, circa 1952), but still funny.

"I'm going to miss Quinn," Wells said. "I know he was a bit of a rake, but he made me smile."

"Where've you been?" I asked. "Lunch date?"

"That's what I told the others. The truth is, I went to my podiatrist." He looked down at his feet encased in orthopedic shoes. "These old dogs are giving out on me."

Standing there in the harsh sunlight, I could see that his face was crisscrossed with wrinkles. He had to be well into his seventies. Maybe even his eighties. If thirty-six was old in Hollywood, poor Wells was practically mummified.

As we started walking towards the Writers' Building, I remembered what he said about wanting to take me to dinner. Maybe I'd take him up on his offer. He knew all the actors on the show. Maybe he could help shed some light on the murder.

"Hey, Wells," I said. "You still up for dinner some time?"

"Why, of course, my dear." His face lit up eagerly. "But what about Duane?"

Duane? Who the heck was Duane?

"Your fiance," Wells said, as if reading my thoughts.

"Oh. Right. Duane. He won't mind. Besides, he's busy right now with an important case."

"An important case?"

"Yes, my fiance's an attorney."

Heck, if I was going to be engaged, I might as well do it right.

"You sure he won't mind?"

"No, he never minds when I go out with *friends*."

Notice the slight emphasis on "friends"—just in case Wells had any ideas about putting the make on me.

"I don't suppose you're free tonight?" he said.

Little did he know that I was free every night for the next three hundred and sixty-five nights.

"Sure," I said. "I'm free."

We agreed to meet at a French joint out in Santa Monica, the place he'd told me about, the one with the great *pommes frites*.

"Till tonight," he said.

Then he blew me a kiss.

Uh-oh. What did I tell you? I smelled trouble in Codger City. To quote Mr. Goldman: Just because there's snow on top, doesn't mean the fire's out down below.

Chapter Fourteen

Kandi barely made a dent in her Shake-a-Salad. She was still too depressed to eat, a condition I'm sad to say I've never experienced.

So I ate her salad as well as my own. With extra dressing, if you must know. I tried to cheer her up with my Helga adventures, but she just lay limply on the sofa, smiling a weak smile, very Camille-on-her-deathbed.

I told her about my upcoming dinner with Wells and how I planned to pump him for information.

"You're going on a *date* with Wells Dumont?" She sat up, her eyes wide with disbelief.

"It's not a real date. We're just having dinner."

"That's what's known as a *dinner date*, Jaine. What if he gets fresh?"

"Don't be silly. He's not going to get fresh."

"What if he tries to kiss you and his dentures come loose?"

"What makes you think he wears dentures?"

"I don't know. I'm just guessing. The guy went to high school with Abe Lincoln, for crying out loud."

"Wells is not going to try and kiss me," I said with an assurance I didn't feel.

"And what about the other suspects?" she asked. "Are you going to try and talk to them, too?"

"Sure," I said. "As soon as I can."

Which turned out to be a lot sooner than I expected. Because who should I run into on my way to the ladies' room after lunch, but one of my prime suspects—Audrey, the woman scorned.

"Hi, Audrey," I chirped.

She smiled coolly. "Oh. Hello, Jaine."

I followed her into the ladies' room, where she bypassed the stalls and headed straight for the mirror. Just as I suspected: The Ice Queen probably never went to the bathroom. I, on the other hand, had to take a tinkle badly, but somehow it didn't seem very professional to conduct my investigation from a toilet stall. So I joined her at the row of sinks where she was fluffing her already perfect hair.

"What a tragedy about Quinn," I said, fluffing my unruly mop.

I saw her jaw tighten.

"Yes, it was," she managed to say. "A terrible tragedy."

Why did I get the feeling she'd had hangnails that were more tragic to her than Quinn's death?

"I still can't believe someone hated him enough to poison him," I went on.

"It's not so hard to believe," she said, applying lipstick with the expertise of a Clinique saleslady. "Quinn had a lot of enemies."

"Yes," I said, "I imagine he did."

With you at the top of the list.

It occurred to me that I couldn't go on fluffing my hair forever. I needed something else to do. I rummaged in my purse and found a lip liner.

"Interesting color," Audrey said, as I started to put it on.

I looked at my reflection in the mirror, and realized to my dismay that it wasn't a lip liner I'd fished from my purse—but an eyebrow pencil.

"Yes," I smiled wanly. "Brown's all the rage this year. I read it in *Elle*."

Damn. Now I'd have to spend the rest of the afternoon with Burnt Ermine lips. Oh, well. I couldn't worry about that now. I had an investigation to conduct.

"When I think of that scene in Muffy's bedroom the other day," I said, shaking my head somberly. "Imagine. Taking advantage of poor Vanessa like that."

Audrey laughed a bitter "hah." When she did, I could smell the distinct aroma of wine on her breath. Something told me Stan hadn't been the only one drinking at lunch that day.

"Poor Vanessa?" she said, her tongue clearly loosened by her lunchtime booze. "Give me a break. The little whore would screw a hatrack."

At which point, we heard the sound of a toilet flushing.

One of the stall doors opened with a bang, and guess who came strutting out? Bingo if you guessed Vanessa.

She walked up to Audrey, popping a piece of Juicy Fruit in her mouth.

"Better a hatrack than Stan," she said.

Then she walked out the door, her head held high, her tush swaying, not bothering to wash her hands.

Audrey's jaws were clenched tighter than a vise.

I had no idea whether or not Audrey Miller killed Quinn Kirkland. But from the murderous look in her eyes, I got the feeling she was fully capable of it.

Audrey's tête-à-tête with Vanessa left her in a pissy mood. She spent the rest of the afternoon trashing my ideas with comments like: "It's an interesting joke, Jaine, except for one thing. It's not funny."

Ouch.

Kandi fared little better. And poor Stan. At one point,

after he'd belched some particularly noxious gin fumes, she turned to him and said: "Sober up, will you? One more drink, and you can rent yourself out as a distillery."

So nobody was shedding any tears when Audrey called it a day at five o'clock and sent us on our way.

Kandi wished me luck on my date with Wells and headed off to yet another emergency session with her shrink. If she kept this up, the guy was going to name a couch after her.

I drove home, stopping off at the supermarket to pick up tuna for Prozac. Bumblebee, packed in water. The most expensive stuff they've got. I told myself I was insane. I should have been buying cat food, or at the very least, Starkist, which was on sale two-for-one.

What can I say? I was blinded by guilt.

I headed for the checkout counter with twenty bucks worth of tuna in my cart. Not to mention a couple of cans of fancy Chinook salmon and a sackful of catnip. Remind me never to have kids; they'd be spoiled rotten before they ever made it out of the crib.

I was just pulling up in front of my duplex when I saw Lance coming out of his apartment. Quickly, I ducked down out of sight. I knew he'd ask me if I'd given *If The Shoe Fits* to Audrey, and I didn't have the energy to lie about it.

I was crouched down, looking at the floor of my car, littered with ancient McDonald's ketchup packets, when I heard:

"Hey, Jaine, what're you doing down there?"

Damn. It was Lance.

"Hi," I said, banging my head against the dashboard. "I dropped this."

I held up one of the ketchup packets, grinning sheepishly.

"So?" Lance asked. "Did you give your boss my treatment?"

"No, not yet," I said, hoisting myself up. "But I'll give it to her tomorrow, I promise."

"That's great, Jaine. Really. I can't tell you how much I appreciate this. Not many people would be as generous as you."

Oh, jeez. If he only knew the truth, that I'd come *this-close* to tossing his treatment into the commissary dumpster.

"It's nothing, Lance," I said. "Really."

"You're a good friend," he said, nodding solemnly. Then he waved good-bye and headed off to his car.

I sat staring at my ketchup packet, filled with guilt. Between Lance and Prozac, I'd generated enough of the stuff to fuel a convention of Jewish mothers.

What sort of a rat was I, anyway? What would be so horrible about giving Lance's treatment to Audrey? So what if she didn't like it? She couldn't possibly hold me responsible for something Lance had written, could she?

I could always leave it on her desk anonymously. Yes, that's what I'd do. That way, if she hated it, she couldn't blame me.

I headed up the path to my apartment, feeling a lot better.

"Prozac, honey," I called out as I let myself into my apartment, "look what Mommy brought. Tuna! Packed in water, just the way you like it."

Prozac looked up from where she was pawing my new Donna Karan pantyhose.

"Prozac," I wailed. "How could you? Do you realize how much those pantyhose cost?"

Prozac yawned in my face, devoid of remorse, clearly not giving a flying fig about my pantyhose.

"Well," I huffed, "if you think I'm giving you Bumblebee white meat tuna, you're sadly mistaken. It's Friskies fishguts for you, young lady. And don't go looking at me all wide-eyed and innocent. I'm not backing down.

It's high time I exercised a little discipline around here."

I marched into the kitchen and opened a can of fishguts. Prozac wandered in, sniffed dismissively, and walked back out again.

"Don't eat it," I shouted after her. "See if I care."

With that, I swept into the bedroom to get ready for my dinner date with Wells. Yes, indeed. It was time I showed that cat who was boss.

Fifteen minutes later, I was coiffed and spritzed and ready to go. I grabbed my car keys and was heading for the front door when Prozac came bounding over to my side. She looked up at me with enormous green eyes and rubbed against my ankles, the queen of adorable.

"I know what you're up to," I told her, "and it's not going to work. I will not cave in. No Bumblebee, and I mean it."

And you'll be happy to know that I stuck to my word. I said I wouldn't give her any tuna, and I didn't. No way. Absolutely not.

I gave her the salmon instead.

La Petite Auberge was a tiny French bistro in Santa Monica, popular with the AARP crowd. Wells and I sat at a checkerboard-sized table, surrounded by seniors finishing their Early Bird Specials. Lots of old guys in plaid pants and white-haired ladies with loose jowls and tight perms.

It was the kind of place where dinners come with soup and salad and the beverage of your choice. Unfortunately they didn't have the beverage of my choice: a double Beefeater martini on the rocks. So I settled for a watery French chardonnay.

When our waitress had taken our orders (*coq au vin* for Wells, duck *à l'orange* for me, and chocolate mousse for dessert), Wells turned to me and said: "So, Jaine. Tell me all about yourself."

"Well—" I began. But I never made it to Syllable Two.

"You remind me so much of a young Joan Plowright," Wells interrupted.

Joan Plowright? Wasn't she the pudgy lady who always played somebody's elderly aunt in Merchant-Ivory movies? Yikes, I told myself, I really had to go on a diet. Just as soon as I finished my duck *à l'orange* and chocolate mousse.

"I knew Joan back when she and I were starring in *All's Well That Ends Well* at Stratford-upon-Avon. Oh, those were the days . . . !"

And he was off and running down memory lane. He talked his way through the soup and the salad and the duck and the coq. I heard all about his life in show biz, starting with the early days working as a magician in London. I heard how he got his first acting gig at the Old Vic, and how he went on to play all the major Shakespearean roles. I heard about how he and his dearly departed wife started their own repertory theater in Boise, Idaho, and how Larry Olivier said he was the best Macbeth he ever saw, and how he knew Judi Dench when she was knee high to a cricket wicket, and blah, blah, blah, blah, until my eyes were practically spinning in my head.

Every once in a while I tried to get in a word edgewise, but it was a lost cause, like a guppy trying to impregnate a whale. Wells was in the middle of a story about playing Scrabble with Sir John "Goodie" Gielgud, when I let my mind wander back to the scene in the Miracle ladies' room.

I remembered the murderous look in Audrey's eyes when Vanessa said that a hatrack would be more fun in bed than Stan. Of course, I had to admit Vanessa was probably right. What with Stan's prodigious liquor consumption, I had a hard time picturing him in the performing mode.

What the heck were Stan and Audrey doing together, anyway? Such an unlikely couple. But the world is full of unlikely couples. Why two people are attracted to each other is one of life's great mysteries. A mystery almost as puzzling as how a two-ounce bag of potato chips can make me gain five pounds. I was sitting there, pondering these and other imponderables, and watching an old lady at the next table cram a half-dozen dinner rolls into her purse, when I became aware that Wells had finally shut up and was looking at me questioningly.

"Jaine?"

Oh, dear. He'd probably just asked me something, and I had no idea what it was.

"Sorry," I said, with an apologetic smile. "I guess I drifted off a little."

"That's all right," he said. "I don't blame you. I'm afraid I've been talking too much. I do that a lot nowadays. Guess it comes from living alone."

I knew exactly what he meant. If I didn't have Prozac to talk to, I'd probably be telling strangers at bus stops about my bad hair days.

"I wasn't this bad," he said, "when Jessica was alive."

"Jessica?"

"My wife." He looked down at the gold wedding band he still wore on his finger. "She passed away ten years ago."

I only hoped she didn't die waiting for him to finish one of his stories.

"So tell me," he said, "what's a lovely young woman doing having dinner with an old coot like me?"

"Actually," I said, "I wanted to ask you some questions. You see, the police think Kandi may have been responsible for Quinn's death—"

"Preposterous!" Wells said, indignant.

"Anyhow, I'm doing a little investigating, to try and figure out who the real killer is."

"Investigating?" His bushy white eyebrows rose in disbelief. "Like a private eye?"

"Sort of. Last year, I helped the police solve a murder in Westwood."

"Did you really? Why, that reminds me of the time I played the inspector in J.B. Priestley's *An Inspector Calls*. Marvelous play. We ran Standing Room Only for eighteen months. Oh, dear," he said, catching himself, "I'm doing it again, aren't I? One of these days, I'm going to have to have my jaws wired shut. So, tell me, what can I do to help?"

"I was hoping you might have seen something the night of the murder. Something suspicious, or out of the ordinary."

"No, not really," he said. "Most of the time, I'm afraid, I was chewing poor Zach's ear off, just as I've done with you tonight. I'm sure he was relieved when I left him to do my soliloquy."

"Do you know where Zach went when you left him?"

"No. He said something about trying to find an aspirin."

Mmm. I couldn't help wondering if he went looking for it in the prop room.

"Can you think of anyone who might have wanted to kill Quinn?"

"Not really. Quinn had his share of detractors, but I don't think anyone disliked him enough to kill him."

"Oh," I said, not bothering to hide my disappointment.

"Wait a minute," he said. "I've got an idea. Perhaps his wife did it."

"His wife?"

"The spouse is the first person the police suspect in

homicides. I learned that when I guest-starred on *Columbo*. It was the episode where the wealthy psychiatrist murders his blackmailing lover. Maybe you've seen it? The *Los Angeles Times* said my performance as the psychiatrist was 'devilishly effective.' "

Whatever made me think this guy was going to be any help? I'd have been better off questioning Prozac.

"Actually," I said, steamrolling past *Columbo*, "Quinn's wife was in New York the night of the murder."

"Pity," Wells sighed, disappointed.

"Aside from Quinn's wife," I said, "can you think of anyone else who might have wanted to kill him?"

"No," he said, "I really can't. Murder's such a drastic act. It's one thing to do it on stage, another thing entirely to do it in real life."

On that philosophical note, our chocolate mousses arrived. I ate every last speck of mine, and most of his, while Wells told me about the time he went skinny-dipping with Dame May Whitty.

At last the check came. Wells insisted on treating me. I let him. I thought of it as combat pay.

He walked me out to my Corolla and waited until I was safely strapped inside.

"Ah," he sighed, "if I were only twenty years younger. . . ."

Was he kidding? He'd still be old enough to be my really old father.

I smiled weakly and thanked him for a lovely evening. Then I drove off into the night, wondering how many calories there were in two chocolate mousses.

YOU'VE GOT MAIL!

TO: Jausten
FROM: Daddyo
SUBJECT: They can't fool me!

Your mom has hidden the love oil. I went out to her
car yesterday to look for it, but it was gone. She's
probably got it stashed away at that sleazeball
Koskovalis's condo. Your mother and John "Kinky"
Koskovalis think they can fool me, but they can't. I'm
on to them both. Although I must say it's him I blame.
After all, your mother is a very impressionable
woman. He's obviously taking advantage of her. Every
time I think of your mother in his greasy arms, I feel
like beating the guy to a pulp.

PS. This morning I caught your mother trying to slip
St. John's Wort into my Wheatena!

TO: Jausten
FROM: Shoptillyoudrop
SUBJECT: Worried about you

Good heavens! I just heard about the murder on your
show! It's all over the news. Jaine, dear, please be
careful. I don't like the idea of your working where a
murder has taken place. And poor Anthony Quinn!
Imagine, him being poisoned like that. I just adored
him in Zorba the Greek.

TO: Shoptillyoudrop
FROM: Jausten

Don't worry, Mom. I'll be fine.
And PS. The actor who died was Quinn Kirkland, not
Anthony Quinn.

TO: Jausten
FROM: Shoptillyoudrop

Oh, dear. I'm having so much trouble with names
lately. I'd be worried about it, if I weren't already so
worried about your father. Yesterday, he bought a
punching bag, and he's been out in the garage all
morning "training." Heaven knows for what!

TO: Jausten
FROM: Daddyo
SUBJECT: Advice for my Lamb Chop

Jaine, lamb chop. Listen to your daddy, and quit your
job immediately! I don't trust any of these show business people. And now that there's been a murder in
your studio, I don't think it's a safe place to be. Well,
gotta go. I've got something very important I've got to
take care of.

TO: Jausten
FROM: Shoptillyoudrop

Your father's just slammed out of the house to, as he
put it, "avenge his honor." Oh, dear. What on earth
does that mean?

Chapter
Fifteen

On Tuesday, we auditioned frogs.

I'm not kidding. Audrey wanted to make sure the frog we used in "Muffy's Revenge" could ribbit on cue. So we spent an entire morning in the conference room as a parade of animal trainers brought in their little green friends.

Do you know how much money Stan and Audrey were getting paid to do this? Seven figures, not including residuals. And inner-city teachers are making zilch. Go write your congressman.

At one point Audrey lost her cool when one of the frogs jumped up on her lap.

"Don't do that again," she said, narrowing her eyes at the wayward amphibian.

And he didn't. Audrey's that intimidating.

After several hours rating amphibians, we finally selected the lead frog and five stand-ins. And then we broke for lunch.

"Guess what," Kandi said, when we got back to our office. "My new agent called me this morning."

"The kid in the mailroom?"

She nodded. "He thinks he can get me a movie-of-the-week."

"That's great! And you said you'd never work again."

But Kandi seemed strangely unenthused.

"So why aren't you doing handsprings?" I asked.

"I'll tell you why. Because the movie's called *Unjustly Jailed.*"

Uh-oh. Cancel the champagne and caviar.

"His exact words were: 'The sitcom scene's looking pretty bleak right now, Kandi, but I think I can get you a movie if they arrest you.' "

She plopped down on the sofa with a groan.

"Between the movie-of-the-week and Ramon's multimillion-dollar lawsuit, I should be in great shape when they finally let me out on parole."

"Don't be silly," I said. "You're not going to jail."

"Yeah, right. Just remember to bake me a cake with a file in it. Make it a fudge cake with white icing. That's one good thing about prison. I won't have to worry about calories."

"Kandi, I swear. You're not going to jail."

"I'll believe it when you find the killer. Speaking of which, how'd it go with Wells last night?"

"Not very productive," I admitted.

"Oh." She sank even deeper into the sofa.

"Cheer up, kiddo. This is just the beginning of my investigation."

"Oh? Who are you going to talk to next?"

Actually, I didn't have the slightest idea who I was going to talk to next. But I couldn't let Kandi know that.

"Uh . . . Vanessa," I said, vamping. "In fact, I'm going over to talk to her right now."

I got up and headed for the door, as if I actually knew what I was doing.

"Lots of luck," she said, wearily.

"Can I bring you back something for lunch?"

"Nah," she sighed. "I'll just suck on some Valium."

*   *   *

I made my way across the lot, past the Miracle roller coaster, where hapless tourists were screaming in terror, no doubt wishing they'd kept up the payments on their life insurance policies. Over on Santa Monica Boulevard, the hookers were in full flower, shaking their fannies at the johns cruising by.

I hadn't told Kandi about the Sturm und Drang going on with my parents; she had troubles enough of her own. But frankly, I was pretty damn worried. What the heck was Daddy doing working out with a punching bag? And what was all that nonsense about "avenging his honor"? Had all those years of hanging around strange cooking appliances somehow affected his thought processes? Lord knows what those contraptions were made of. Maybe some electrical currents were leaking out and turning his brain into applesauce.

Just when I was having visions of Daddy locked up behind bars in a high-security mental institution, I heard someone call my name. I turned and saw Dale Burton grinning at me.

"Hi, Jaine," he said, running his fingers through his thick shock of sandy hair. (What was it about these actors? Didn't any of them ever have bad hair? Was I the only one on the lot, other than Helga, with hair that frizzed in the rain?)

"How's it going?" he asked.

"Fine."

If you don't count the fact that my best friend is a murder suspect, and my father's going bonkers.

"I'm throwing a little party Thursday night, and I thought you and Kandi could stop by."

Wow. Talk about tacky. What was the theme going to be: *Quinn's Dead; Let's Party*?

"I know it might seem a little tacky having a party so soon after Quinn's death, but I can't cancel the caterers without losing my deposit."

"No," I lied, "it's not tacky at all."

"So can you come?"

"Sure, I'd love to."

And that was no lie. It would be a perfect opportunity for me to do some more nosing around.

"Stan and Audrey will be there," he said, obviously thrilled to have them on his guest list. "It'll be great. We'll schmooze, booze, and knock around story ideas. See you then," he said, shooting his finger at me like a gun.

Then he bounded off toward the commissary.

If Dale Burton was in mourning for Quinn, he was doing a hell of a job hiding it.

I knocked on the door to Vanessa's trailer, not exactly brimming with confidence. The kid had all the warmth and charm of a prison warden. I only hoped I'd be able to get her to answer some questions.

"Who is it?" Vanessa called out.

"It's me. Jaine."

"Jane? I don't know any Jane."

I was heartened to see what a great impression I'd made on her.

"Jaine Austen," I said.

I heard her whispering to someone inside the trailer. She was probably busy calling Security.

"I wrote this week's script," I said.

Or, as you so tactfully put it, this week's piece of shit.

"Oh, right. Get the door," she barked to whoever was in the room with her.

A mousy, middle-aged woman with watery blue eyes answered the door. She smiled tentatively.

"Come in, won't you?"

Oh, well. At least someone in the trailer had manners.

Vanessa was stretched out on a mauve chenille sofa

which, unlike our vermin-infested model, looked like it was fresh from the showroom. She sat pecking at a salad and reading *Vogue*, a pair of oversized hornrimmed glasses perched on her tiny nose. The big glasses on her fine boned face made her look oddly vulnerable.

"Hey, Jaine," she said, "you got a cigarette on you?"

"No, I'm afraid I don't smoke."

She turned to her mousy assistant.

"Why the hell can't you ever remember to get me cigarettes?"

"Sorry," the mouse said, eyes downcast, looking as if she wished the floor would swallow her right up, "I didn't realize you'd run out."

"And this salad," Vanessa said, plucking a glob of cheese from the greens, "it's got blue cheese. How many times do I have to tell you, I hate blue cheese?"

The mouse sprinted over to retrieve the offending salad.

"Shall I get you another one, dear?" she asked, desperate to please.

Remind me never to get a job as a personal assistant in Hollywood. It's slave labor—without the room and board.

"Oh, forget it," Vanessa said. "Just get me a Hershey bar and a carton of Virginia Slims."

Why did I have the feeling that it was the Hershey bar she'd wanted all along, and that she'd gone through the charade of ordering a salad just to drive her poor assistant crazy?

The mouse grabbed a worn cardigan sweater and scampered out the door.

"And hurry it up, willya, Mom? I'm starving."

Mom??? The mouse was Vanessa's mom? How heartwarming.

Vanessa popped a piece of Juicy Fruit into her mouth.

"So what do you want?" she said, wasting no time on idle chitchat.

"I'd like to interview you for a cover story I'm doing for *TV Guide*. On Teen Stars."

Yes, I know it was an outrageous lie, but if I told her I was investigating Quinn's murder, she might not want to talk to me. This way, I'd appeal to her vanity. There was no way she was going to turn down a cover story in *TV Guide*. I was feeling quite proud of myself for thinking up such a clever ploy, when Vanessa popped her gum and said:

"Bullshit."

Huh?

"*TV Guide* never gives cover stories to freelancers."

Wow. Somebody wasn't half as dumb as she looked.

"You're investigating Quinn's murder."

"How did you know?"

"Wells told us at rehearsal. Besides, I read in the papers about how you solved that murder in Westwood last year."

I blinked in amazement. Not that she knew about the case, but that she'd actually read a newspaper. It looked like she had more than a few brain cells bouncing around in that lovely head of hers.

"You're right," I confessed. "I am doing some investigating. Right now Kandi seems to be high on the cops' suspect list, and I'm trying to get her off the hook. So is it okay if I ask you some questions?"

"I don't care," she shrugged, trying her best to look nonchalant.

"You have any idea who might've killed Quinn?"

"Of course. It was Audrey."

"What makes you say that?"

"Oh, come on, you saw how pissed off she was when she caught Quinn and me in the sack together. Quinn told me she threatened to get rid of him. He never figured she meant permanently."

"Did he tell you he'd been having an affair with her?" I asked.

"Sure."

"And you didn't mind?"

"Hey. I'm a big girl." She stuck her chin out defiantly, like a B actress in a film noir. "And it's not like I wasn't screwing around with other guys."

She was trying so hard to be tough. But I wasn't convinced. I don't care how many guys she claimed to have slept with (and I suspected there weren't that many), she was still just a kid. A kid who might have been devastated to learn that her grown-up lover had been cheating on her. Maybe Quinn had been as callous with Vanessa as he'd been with Kandi, and she went a little bonkers. After all, unlike Kandi and the rest of us mere mortals, Vanessa Duffy wasn't used to being rejected.

And maybe she assuaged her hurt feelings with a dose of rat poison.

It all made sense. The way I saw it, any kid capable of treating her mother like a scullery maid could easily be capable of murder.

I asked her some routine questions and got some routine answers. She'd seen nothing and heard nothing the night of the murder.

I thanked her for her time and was just about to leave when her mother came rushing in, breathless.

"Here are your cigarettes, dear, and your Hershey bar."

The last thing I heard as I headed out the door was:

"Shit, Mom. It's got nuts. You know I hate nuts."

Chapter
Sixteen

I started back to the office, but I hadn't gone very far when I stopped in my tracks. There, standing before me, was Quinn's trailer, festooned with big yellow *Do Not Enter* police banners.

Now I know what you're thinking: Any sane person would have read the banners and thought, *Hey, maybe I'd better not enter*. But not me. I decided to break in.

Actually, it's not nearly as reckless as it sounds. I looked around the backlot and saw there wasn't a soul in sight. The coast was most definitely clear. How tough could it be to nip in and look for clues?

I sprinted up the steps and tried the door. It was locked, of course. But I wasn't going to let that stop me. I reached in my purse and got out my Bloomingdale's charge card. I'd seen TV private eyes open doors this way a million times. Surely it would work for me.

I was standing there, jiggling my Bloomie's card, wondering if I'd remembered to pay last month's bill, when suddenly I looked up and saw a cop approaching. A big burly cop with deltoids the size of watermelons.

Gad, she was scary.

What the heck was I going to tell her—that I thought Bloomie's had opened a branch in Quinn's trailer? My mind was racing, trying to think up a plausible lie, when I saw her reach into her back pocket. Good Lord, she was going for her gun! She was going to shoot me! She'd probably claim I threatened her, that she fired in self-defense. Any minute now, my blood-soaked body would be sprawled on the Miracle lot. Just another victim of police brutality.

I was frantically trying to remember the words to the Twenty-Third Psalm, praying that God would let me into heaven in spite of all my unpaid parking tickets, when I saw that it wasn't a gun the cop was taking out of her back pocket, but a script! Then I noticed heavy pancake makeup on her face. Thank heavens. She wasn't a cop . . . she was an actor! Probably a member of the *PMS Squad*.

She ambled past the trailer, studying her script, totally unaware of my existence.

After waiting for my heart to stop bouncing around in my chest, I decided to abandon my plan to break into Quinn's trailer. It wasn't worth a coronary. But when I tried to pull out my Bloomie's card, it was stuck. Oh, great. Now the police would find my credit card in the door. This whole thing was turning into a major nightmare. I was yanking at the card, swearing a blue streak, when I heard a clicking noise, and the door swung open.

I suppose I should've grabbed my card and run, but I couldn't resist the lure of that open door. I tiptoed in and looked around.

Like Vanessa's trailer, Quinn's was furnished quite nicely, with tasteful modern furniture. I don't know what I expected. Early Brothel, perhaps.

The first thing I noticed was a Steuben bowl, filled to the brim with chocolate kisses. How fitting, I thought, that the studio lover should have kisses in his trailer. Seeing the chocolates reminded me that I hadn't had lunch, and that I was hungry. Yes, I know I was on a diet, and the last thing I needed was more chocolate clinging to my thighs, but I reached for one anyway. For crying out loud, it's only twenty-five calories. And all I had was one.

Okay, okay. So I had twelve. Are you happy now?

I was just unwrapping my thirteenth kiss when it occurred to me: A) Not only was I eating potential evidence, but B) What if Quinn's killer had also poisoned the kisses?

Aaack. Suddenly I felt a searing pain in my chest. Good heavens, I was right. The kisses were poisoned! For the second time in less than five minutes, I was about to cash in my chips. I was clutching my chest, wondering what sort of turnout I'd get at my funeral, when relief came with a ladylike belch.

It was only gas.

I sank down onto Quinn's sofa, weak with relief. I'd really have to do something about my tendency to panic, if I ever intended to have any success as a private eye. While I was on the sofa, I decided to check under the cushions. I might find a valuable piece of evidence the cops had overlooked. Either that, or some spare change. As it turns out, all I came up with was a fistful of lint.

I rummaged around the rest of the trailer, but found nothing of interest except for a pair of leopard-print thong briefs and a T-shirt that said *Love Instructor: First Lesson Free*.

I was just about to call it quits when I decided to give the sofa another try. As the only bedlike surface in the room, it had probably seen a lot of action. I squeezed my fingers into the seams of the sofa, deeper than I'd poked them before.

And this time it paid off. I felt something. Hard and smooth. Like a pencil. I pulled it out and saw that it wasn't a pencil but a tortoise-shell hair ornament, shaped like a chopstick. It looked vaguely familiar. Where had I seen it before? Then I remembered: It was the same tortoise-shell ornament I'd seen nestled in Bianca's hair.

Holy Moses. So I'd been right the other day. It looked like Bianca had been sleeping with Quinn, after all. Was there a woman on the planet—except for me and Helga—who hadn't been sleeping with the guy?

I gazed down at the chopstick and wondered: Was it possible that Bianca was the one who sprinkled the rat poison onto Quinn's donut?

But according to Detective Incorvia, Bianca had an alibi. She'd been with Danny, the production assistant, the entire time the prop room was empty. But had she really? I could've sworn I saw Danny running around backstage while I was talking with Wells and Zach. What if he and Bianca hadn't been together? What if she'd made a deal with him? *We'll each say we were together; that way the cops will leave us alone.* Not that she was anywhere near the prop room, she'd assure Danny. *But why have the cops bother us with questions? We don't want to wind up like Kandi, do we, with our pictures splashed across the papers and our careers in the toilet?*

Yes, Bianca had definitely wormed her way onto my list of suspects. Which by now was growing faster than mushrooms in the rain.

There was Audrey (the scorned lover) and Stan (the jealous husband) and Vanessa (the jaded jailbait) and Dale (the cell phone maniac whose career had sky-rocketed since the demise of his rival).

And what about Vanessa's mom? Maybe she killed Quinn. Maybe she couldn't stand the thought of a smarmy, middle-aged man with thong underwear and salacious T-shirts boffing her daughter. True, Vanessa's mom had seemed about as murderous as a Carmelite nun, but who knew what was lurking under her docile facade? Jeffrey Dahlmer was a mild-mannered guy, until you let him loose with a carving knife.

I wiped my fingerprints from the chopstick and left it out on the sofa, where I hoped the cops would discover it.

Then I tiptoed out the door. But not before grabbing one last kiss for the road.

Chapter Seventeen

"The butler did it!" Mr. Goldman said.

It was Tuesday night and I was back at the Shalom Retirement Home, trying to conduct my memoir-writing class. But the only thing my students wanted to talk about was the murder.

"What butler?" Mrs. Pechter said. "There was no butler in the show."

"Sure there was," said Mr. Goldman. "The guy with the English accent."

"Wells Dumont doesn't play a butler," I explained. "He's Muffy's neighbor."

"A fact which you'd know," huffed Mrs. Rubin, "if you'd actually watched the show instead of flirting with the wardrobe lady."

"She had the hots for me," Mr. Goldman said, direct from Delusionland.

"It said in the *Enquirer* that the little girl, Vanessa Whatshername, was shtupping Quinn Kirkland," Mrs. Pechter said. "Can you imagine? If I was her mother, I'd have killed him with my bare hands."

"Okay, class," I broke in. "It's time to get started."

"What are you doing reading a rag like the *Enquirer*?" Mrs. Rubin asked.

"I found it in the laundry room. And look who's talking. I'm not the one who watches Jerry Springer."

"Jerry's shows happen to be very educational."

"So who wants to read me an essay?"

"I say the murderer was Audrey Miller. I heard on *Access Hollywood* she was shtupping him, too."

"You watch *Access Hollywood?* That's worse than Jerry Springer."

"I say it was the other actor. Dale Burton. The one who plays Muffy's father."

"Oh, please. He couldn't have done it. He's such a sweet man. He looks just like my son Ronny."

"*Entertainment Tonight* says now that Quinn Kirkland is dead, Dale Burton's part is bigger than ever."

"So how about it, class? Who's got an essay for me?"

"I hate to say this, Jaine, darling. But I think it was your friend Kandi. She was the only one who was seen in the prop room."

"Mrs. Zahler," I said. "how about you? Why don't you read us what you've got?"

But Mrs. Zahler had other plans.

"I say it was accidental food poisoning," she said.

"I'll never forget the time I ate a bad clam in the Marina," Mrs. Pechter chimed in. "I didn't think I'd live to tell about it."

"That's nothing. My cousin got a perforated ulcer from a piece of glass in his pizza."

"My sister-in-law once found a worm in a Caesar's salad."

"I still say the butler did it."

For the second week in a row, we read no essays. The murder was the topic of choice. Suspects were discussed. Motives delved into. After much debate, everyone agreed on one thing: Never, ever, order tuna salad in a Mexican restaurant.

* * *

I drove home from Shalom, my mind whirling with suspects. It was all so damn frustrating. The more I learned, the less I knew.

I wished there was some way I could tell Detective Incorvia about Bianca's hair ornament. But if I told him, he'd want to know what I was doing in Quinn's trailer. Call me paranoid, but I had a feeling that breaking and entering a dead man's trailer was definitely a police no-no.

What I needed was a bath. Yes, a steamy soak in a strawberry-scented tub would feel absolutely marvelous right now. I'd lower the lights, pour myself a teensy tad of chardonnay, and soak myself till my muscles were the consistency of Campbell's chicken noodles.

I pulled up in front of my duplex, happy to see that Lance's lights were out. I still hadn't left his treatment on Audrey's desk, and I didn't want him asking me about it.

I crept past his place, just in case he was lying in wait for me, and let myself into my apartment. My answering machine was blinking. Wow. One whole message. How popular can a gal get?

It was Detective Incorvia.

"Ms. Austen, I just wanted to let you know. We found Kandi Tobolowski's fingerprints all over the prop room."

"So?" I shouted at the machine. "That doesn't mean she killed Quinn. All it means is she was stupid enough to go snooping around the damn prop room, looking for stethoscopes."

"Oh, and by the way," Incorvia's voice continued, "do you think it's okay if a script runs more than a hundred and twenty pages?"

I deleted his message with an angry jab of my finger. When the heck was he going to put some effort into finding the real murderer? I was surprised he even remembered there'd been a murder, what with having to deal with the really important issue of his page count.

I headed over to Prozac, who was curled up on the sofa, napping on my toothbrush. She barely glanced at me. She was sulking, still pissed at me for abandoning her.

I gave her a conciliatory kiss, which she returned with a smelly Bumblebee yawn.

I got undressed and ran the water for my bath, tossing in a generous fistful of bath salts. Then I poured myself that teensy tad of chardonnay. (Okay, so it was a Flintstone's orange juice glass, and I filled it all the way to the top of Fred's toga.)

I was just about to step in the tub when I thought: Why not keep a pad and pencil handy in case I had a brainstorm in the tub? Actually, I get some of my best ideas in the tub. The tub is where I came up with one of my most successful ad campaigns (*When You Gotta Go, Go Toiletmasters!*).

Naked as a jaybird, I dashed to the living room and opened the briefcase I'd bought especially for my gig on *Muffy 'n Me*. I thought it gave me a much-needed air of competence. I reached in to grab a legal pad and felt something cold and clammy. I couldn't imagine what it was. A piece of fruit I'd stuck in there and forgotten? I opened the briefcase wider to get a better look when suddenly something green and slimy leaped out.

Want to guess what it was? I'll give you a clue. It had big bulging eyes and was covered with warts.

No, it wasn't my ex-husband. It was a frog.

One of the frogs from the audition had somehow gotten loose and taken up residence in my briefcase. And now it was spronging all over my living room.

Prozac's eyes widened with blood lust. Her old hunting instincts, long confined to attacking my pantyhose, came bubbling to the surface. I could practically read her mind: *Gee, I've always wanted to try frog's legs.* She assumed her attack position, crouched down in a vigilant coil, ready to pounce. I quickly swooped her up in my arms. If I couldn't solve a murder, at least I could prevent one.

I turned and looked for the frog, but now it was nowhere in sight. Damn. Where had it gone?

So there I was, stark naked, roaming around my apartment with a cat in my arms calling, "Here, froggy. Here, froggy!" Which, of course, was the perfect time for the doorbell to ring.

"Jaine, it's me," Lance called from outside my front door. "Wanna gossip?"

"Actually, Lance. I'm stark naked and I've got a frog loose in my apartment."

"Well," he said, miffed. "If you're not in the mood to talk, just say so."

And off he stomped into the night.

Oh, well. I'd explain everything tomorrow. Meanwhile, I had a frog to catch. I locked a howling Prozac in her cat carrier and proceeded to search the apartment.

I looked everywhere, every nook, every cranny, every closet. But the only critters I found were dustbunnies.

I was on my hands and knees, tossing shoes out of my closet, when I glanced down into my new Joan & David leather boots, the ones that cost more money than an economy car. Two beady eyes were staring up at me. I could only assume they belonged to the frog.

"There you are, you little rascal."

I reached in and grabbed it. Not a pleasant experience for either of us. Then I dashed into the living room, where I opened the latch to the cat carrier. Prozac streaked out, and I put the frog inside.

Poor little thing. It looked scared. And probably hungry, too. What the heck do you feed a frog? Lettuce, maybe, and dead flies. I rummaged around in my refrigerator, but all I found was a bottle of garlic-stuffed olives. Definitely not froggie chow. I checked my windowsills for dead flies, but came up empty-handed.

As a last-ditch effort, I put some Bumblebee on a plate and shoved it into the cage. But the frog ignored it.

"A Starkist man, are you?"

Oh, well. I was sure he'd survive until tomorrow. I'd bring him back to the studio, where the casting department would reunite him with his rightful owner.

By now, my bath water was ice cold. So much for brainstorming in the tub. I was too exhausted to think, anyway. I drained the water from the tub and took a quick shower instead. Then I locked the frog in the bathroom, safe from Prozac's deadly clutches.

I crawled into bed and lay there staring at the ceiling. Gad, what a day.

Prozac stood outside the bathroom door, hissing and scratching. She would've sold her soul to get her paws on that frog. *If only there were some way to open the bathroom door*, she was undoubtedly thinking. *Why the heck don't cats have opposable thumbs, anyway?* Or words to that effect.

Yes, Prozac had a major problem on her hands, with absolutely no idea how to solve it.

I knew exactly how she felt.

I woke up the next morning to the sweet sounds of a frog ribbiting.

Prozac had given up her murderous vigil sometime in the middle of the night and was now curled up against my tummy, the picture of innocence. Cats are amazing, aren't they? One minute, they're furry little angels; the next, they're merciless killing machines.

I hoisted myself out of bed and headed for the bathroom, where I performed my morning toilette under the watchful eye of my amphibian houseguest. Then I padded out to the kitchen and rustled up breakfast: Tuna for Prozac, coffee and garlic-stuffed olive for me. Prozac was torn between the tuna and the frog. Which would be tastier? Probably the frog. But you know the old adage: A fish in the hand is worth two frog's legs in the bathroom.

She went for the tuna.

I grabbed my coffee and hurried to the bedroom to throw on some clothes. I wanted to get to the studio as soon as possible before, you'll pardon the expression, the frog croaked.

I was just heading down the path to my car when Lance popped out from his apartment.

"See, Lance?" I held up the cat carrier and showed him the frog. "There really was a frog in my apartment last night."

"I know," he said, a tad on the cranky side. "I heard it ribbiting all night long."

What did I tell you? The man has x-ray hearing.

"So did you give my treatment to Audrey?"

"Yes," I lied. Anything to get him off my back.

"Oh, that's great," he said, the ribbits in the night totally forgotten.

"Don't get your hopes up," I warned him. "Audrey can be a pretty tough critic."

"I just know she's going to love it," Lance said. "I mean, what's not to like?"

Obviously Lance and Mr. Goldman were roommates in Delusionland.

"Yes," I managed to say. "I'm sure she'll love it."

One more lie, and I'd turn into a congressman.

You should have seen the look on Bianca's face when I dropped the frog at her desk.

"Yuck," she said. "How disgusting."

I couldn't tell whether she was talking about the frog or me.

"One of the animal trainers must have left it here yesterday," I said.

Bianca went back to buffing her nails. "You'll have to bring it over to casting. That's not my department."

"No, *you'll* have to bring it to casting, you snotty little bitch. You're the secretary. Running errands *is* your department."

Okay, so that's not exactly what I said. My exact words were, "Okey-dokey."

The casting people were thrilled to see me. Apparently the frog's owner had put in a frantic Missing Amphibian call. They greeted my warty friend with welcoming coos and promised they'd return my carrying case as soon as possible. I bid the frog a fond farewell.

"Don't be a stranger," I said.

He looked at me with an inscrutable expression, which I later learned meant: "I wouldn't step into your new Joan & David boots barefoot if I were you."

"Euuu. How gross." Kandi wrinkled her nose in disgust when I told her about my adventures with Mr. Frog. "Finding a slimy creature lurking in your apartment like that."

"Yeah," I said. "It brought back memories of my marriage."

We were sitting at our desks, eating our morning bagels and cream cheese. That is, I was eating my morning bagel and cream cheese. Kandi, still too depressed to eat, was ignoring hers.

"I wonder how it got in your attache case," she said, absently drawing designs on her cream cheese with the tines of a plastic fork.

"Probably jumped in when nobody was looking."

"Maybe," Kandi said. "Or maybe somebody put it there."

"Why would anyone do something as idiotic as that?"

"You know. As a practical joke."

It hadn't occurred to me before, but maybe someone *had* put the frog in my briefcase. Not as a practical joke, but to make things uncomfortable for me. Maybe that someone was the murderer. Suddenly I felt a tiny stab of fear in the pit of my stomach. Which, I'm ashamed to say, I quickly sedated with Kandi's uneaten bagel.

We spent most of the day writing frog jokes. Then, at about four o'clock, we went down to the stage to see a run-through of my Cinderella script. I say "my" in the loosest sense of the word. At this point, only about five of my original jokes had survived. Which, according to Kandi, isn't bad for a freelance script. I guess that's why so many sitcom writers are on intravenous antidepressants.

Luckily, I'd contributed some new jokes in the rewrites, so my ego wasn't totally destroyed. And the show was looking pretty good. Dale was funnier than I'd ever seen him, and Zach was turning in a lively performance, too. Audrey laughed out loud at some of the gags, and even Stan managed a boozy chuckle. It was hard to believe that less than a week ago, someone had died on that very stage.

After the run-through, the actors went home to loll around and eat bonbons while we writers retired to slave quarters to work on the script. We spent about an hour punching up jokes, and then Audrey called it a day.

Kandi headed off for another session with Dr. Mellman. I decided to hang out in the office until Stan and Audrey left, so I could slip Lance's treatment on Audrey's desk.

Maybe Audrey would read it. Maybe she wouldn't. All I knew is that I promised Lance I'd give it to her. And technically, I was keeping my promise.

I sat at my desk, armed with pad and pencil, determined to make a detailed list of my suspects. I got as far as *My Suspects, By Jaine Austen,* when my mind started wandering.

I couldn't get over how quickly everyone seemed to have forgotten Quinn. It was show business as usual at the studio. People were laughing and joking and back-stabbing as if he'd never existed. I only hoped that when I died I'd be on *somebody's* mind a week later, that I wouldn't be forgotten like yesterday's fad diet.

I was roused from my reverie by the sound of Stan and Audrey shutting their door and heading down the hallway. When I was fairly certain they were gone, I opened my door and peeked out.

Bianca was still at her desk, gabbing on the phone about a party she might or might not decide to go to. Blah, blah, blah, yap, yap, yap. Really, a most annoying person. Finally, she decided to go to the party and hung up. Good. Now maybe she'd move her fanny and go home.

She was gathering her things, unaware that I was spying on her, when her phone rang.

Damn. How long was this call going to drag out?

"Oh, hi, Danny," she smiled. "What's up?" Whatever Danny said wiped the smile from her face. "Oh, come on. You're not going to get all wussy on me, are you? I thought we made a deal. . . . Look, don't do anything until I see you, okay?"

She hung up, looking worried. Then she grabbed her purse and hurried off. Hmmm. Maybe my theory was right. Maybe she *had* made a deal with Danny to supply each other with alibis. It looked like I was getting pretty good at this detective stuff.

Feeling rather proud of myself, I headed next door to the Millers' office with Lance's treatment. But when I tried the door, it was locked. I thought of breaking in with my Bloomie's card, but it wasn't worth the risk.

The cleaning crew would be showing up for work any minute now. I'd have to try again tomorrow.

I turned off the lights and headed out to the parking lot. But not before checking my briefcase for stray amphibians.

Chapter
Eighteen

It was dusk when I left the Writers' Building. The last studio tour of the day was grinding to a halt, and tourists with glazed eyes were heading back to their cars. "Hey," said a plump lady in spandex leggings, "isn't that Zach Levy-Taylor?"

I looked over to where she was pointing, and indeed it was Zach, hitting tennis balls against the wall of the *Muffy* soundstage.

"Ladies and gentlemen, please keep to your right," the tour guide said, keeping his charges away from Miracle's teen heartthrob.

The guide had no jurisdiction over me, however, so I trotted over to Zach's side.

As I stood watching him bat his tennis ball against the soundstage, I couldn't help noticing his tight, tan young body. (Hey, I may have been celibate, but I wasn't dead.)

But in spite of Zach's obvious sexual appeal, he was still just a kid. His long legs were still on the gangly side; and his blond hair, normally spiked into peaks with fistfuls of gel, was flopping boyishly onto his forehead.

These show biz kids, I thought, really do miss out on a lot. This is what Zach should be doing: Playing tennis, skateboarding, joining the stamp club, going to proms.

Not hanging out with paunchy, middle-aged grips with hernias and alimony payments.

"Hey, Zach. How's it going?"

"Oh, hi, Judy," he said, still batting the ball.

"Actually, it's Jaine."

"That's right. Jane Eyre. Like the book."

"No, it's Austen. Jaine Austen. With an 'i.' "

"Gee, I thought Austen was spelled with an 'e.' "

I could see our conversation was rapidly turning into a Marx Brothers routine, so I deftly changed the subject.

"Say, Zach, do you have a minute? I'd like to talk with you."

"What about?"

"Quinn's murder."

For the first time since I started watching him, he missed the ball.

"Oh, yeah," he said, running to get it. "Vanessa told me you were trying to get Kandi off the hook."

"So can I ask you some questions?"

"Sure," he said. "But I don't think I know anything that's going to help you."

"How about we go sit down inside?" I said, gesturing to the stage.

We walked into the cool interior of the soundstage. It looked even larger than usual now that it was empty. Our footsteps echoed as we walked over to Muffy's kitchen set.

Zach went to the kitchen counter and lifted the lid off an old-fashioned cookie jar. He reached inside and pulled out a bottle of scotch. Then he opened it and took a long swig.

So I was wrong about Zach. He was a typical teenager, after all.

"Want some?" he asked, wiping the lip of the bottle on his T-shirt.

"No, thanks." I smiled weakly. "I'll pass."

"So," he said, pulling out one of the kitchen chairs and straddling it backwards. "How can I help you?"

"Did you see anything unusual the night of the murder? Anything at all?"

He plastered a pensive look on his face.

"Nope," he said, "I don't think so. But then, I wasn't really paying attention. Wells had me cornered, and when Wells starts gabbing, I sorta zone out."

"Did you ever find that aspirin?"

"What aspirin?"

"Wells told me you went looking for an aspirin when he went on stage to do his soliloquy."

"Oh, right. I got one from Teri, the makeup lady," he said, shooting me an uneasy glance. "I didn't get it from the prop room, if that's what you're implying."

Oh, my. For an innocent person, he was awfully defensive, *n'est-ce pas?*

"I'm not implying anything, Zach. I was just asking a question. But now that you bring it up, did you happen to see anyone going into the prop room?"

"Only Kandi," he smirked.

Not the answer I wanted.

"Kandi didn't do it, Zach."

"You're probably right," he admitted. "She doesn't seem the type."

"Do you have any idea who might have poisoned Quinn?"

"Hell, no. Everybody loved him."

If I'd been drinking the scotch, I would've choked on it.

"Wait a minute. Surely you're not telling me *you* liked Quinn?"

"Yeah, I did. He was a great guy."

"But what about that scene in rehearsal? You said you wanted to kill him."

"Oh, that," he said dismissively. "That didn't mean anything. I was pissed that day. These things happen all the time on the set. If you were a real TV writer, you'd know that."

Ouch. That one hurt.

"So it didn't bother you that Vanessa was sleeping with Quinn?"

His Malibu tan turned scarlet.

"No, not really."

If this kid was telling the truth, I'd eat Helga's hair net.

"Everyone makes mistakes," he said, oozing sanctimony. "Vanessa made hers, and I'm sure she regrets it."

"Oh? That's not the impression I got when I talked to her. I think she was crazy in love with Quinn. In fact, I think she still is."

Score one for *moi*. Zach glared at me with ill-concealed anger.

"Wow," he said, checking his watch and doing a very bad impression of someone who'd lost track of time. "I didn't realize how late it was. I really gotta go, Judy."

He untangled his legs from the chair rungs and stood up.

"Well, see ya," he said, flashing me what was meant to be a disarming grin. "And good luck on your investigation."

As I watched him walk away, I wondered how on earth he'd ever made it this far in show biz. The kid was one hell of a lousy actor.

So there I was, alone in Muffy's house, like a burglar on a heist. And suddenly, I was overcome by a ridiculous urge to snoop. Of course I knew I wasn't going to find anything. It was a make-believe house, with nothing stored away—except for some scotch in a cookie jar.

Nevertheless, I wandered around, opening empty drawers and peeking into fake closets. I plopped down into the big, overstuffed living-room armchair, the one that Muffy's dad sat in when he watched TV or chewed the fat with Mr. Watkins. I looked out the window onto a painted backdrop of a grassy suburban street. If I squinted my eyes, it almost looked real. Any minute now, I expected Ozzie and Harriet to walk in the front door with tutti-frutti ice cream.

I got up and wandered into Muffy's bedroom, the scene of Vanessa's sexcapade with Quinn. Now it was an innocent teenager's room again, with white lace curtains and fuzzy stuffed animals propped up on a recently dry-cleaned chenille bedspread. I picked up one of the stuffed animals, a soft puppy with big brown glass eyes. I sniffed it. It smelled of Juicy Fruit gum.

Then I reached over to Muffy's white wicker night table and idly pulled out a drawer. Rattling around inside was a half-empty bottle of water and a giant economy-size box of condoms. Strawberry scented, yet. What would they think of next? Chocolate G-strings? I opened the box and saw that there were just a few condoms left. Obviously Vanessa's recent boff-a-thon with Quinn hadn't been the only time she'd used Muffy's bed for X-rated purposes.

I took a closer look at the water bottle and saw that it was Evian. A crazy idea popped into my head. On an impulse, I opened the bottle and sniffed. Just as I suspected:

It was gin.

I sank down on Muffy's bed, dumbstruck.

Did this mean that Stan had been sleeping with Vanessa? While Audrey was cheating on Stan with Quinn, had Stan been cheating on Audrey with Vanessa? Was this one of those unsavory Hollywood daisy chains that you read about in a Jackie Collins novel?

But, no. It couldn't be. I simply couldn't picture Stan and Vanessa in the same bed together. And besides, didn't Vanessa say she'd rather sleep with a hat rack than Stan?

Maybe someone had stolen the bottle from Stan's private stash. After all, Stan's drinking was an open secret. Anyone could have nipped into his office and filched a bottle or two.

By now my head was spinning. I practically need a scorecard to keep track of the sexcapades on the *Muffy* set. And what was worse, I still had absolutely no idea who killed Quinn. The possibilities were endless. There was only one thing to do: Sit down and make a detailed list of my suspects.

I headed back to Muffy's kitchen and took out my legal pad. I cleared a place on the perfectly set kitchen table, and started writing. I'd gotten as far as . . .

My Suspects

. . . when suddenly it occurred to me that I really ought to call Detective Incorvia and tell him about the Evian/gin bottle in Muffy's night table. It might be an important piece of evidence. I grabbed my cell phone and called his office. I got his voice mail. Where the heck was he? Probably at the beach, writing his screenplay.

"Hi, Detective Incorvia. It's Jaine Austen. I've just found something that might interest you. Please call me when you get back."

Now that was taken care of, I could get down to business. I picked up my pen and started writing. I got as far as . . .

My Suspects
By Jaine—

. . . when I realized I was hungry. It had been ages and ages since the puny white-rubber-cheese sandwich I'd had for lunch. From sheer force of habit, I got up and looked in the refrigerator. Of course there was nothing there, except an old script called "Muffy Gets a Zit." I rummaged around the bottom of my purse and found a linty Lifesaver, which I dusted off and popped into my mouth.

Okay, *now* I'd get down to business. I managed to make it to . . .

My Suspects
By Jaine Austen—

. . . when it suddenly dawned on me that I was sitting in the same seat Quinn had been sitting in when he died. Yikes. I was in a Dead Man's Chair.

Instinctively, I leaped up. And it was a good thing I did. For at that very moment, a hundred-pound overhead light came crashing down onto the kitchen table. Just inches from where I had been sitting.

Chapter
Nineteen

I don't know how long I stood there, rigid with fear, staring at the lethal black lump that had landed on Muffy's kitchen table, gouging it like a meteor from outer space. Finally I managed to open my mouth and scream. Louder than I've screamed in my life. Louder, even, than the time I had my first and only bikini wax.

I forced myself to look up into the rafters, but it was too dark to see clearly. For all I knew, someone could have been hiding up there in the shadows of the cat-walks.

At last, one of Miracle's crackerjack security guards came racing into the soundstage. The guard, whose name tag said "Bobby," was a kid, barely past the Clearasil years. With a faceful of freckles and an unruly cowlick, he looked like Dennis the Menace in uniform.

"Gosh," he said, taking in the scene. "What happened?"

"Someone tried to kill me," I shrieked. "Call the police."

"Gee, I can't call the cops, ma'am. Not without authorization."

"Authorization? What authorization?"

And why was he calling me "ma'am"? Did I look that old?

"From Mr. Donnelly."

"Who's Mr. Donnelly?"

"Head of Security."

"Screw Mr. Donnelly," I said. "I'm calling the cops myself."

I was just reaching for my cell phone when a burly guy with a gut the size of a watermelon came puffing onto the stage.

"Hey, Mr. Donnelly," the kid said. "I was just about to call you."

"What the hell is going on here?"

"Someone tried to kill me with a klieg light," I said. "I was sitting at the kitchen table, and the light fell just inches away from where I was sitting. The wires must have been cut."

Donnelly took out his flashlight and shone it up into the rafters.

"Nobody's up there."

"Of course not. Whoever did it wasn't going to stick around and wait for Security to show up."

"What makes you think anyone's trying to kill you, ma'am?"

Why did these idiots keep calling me ma'am? Any minute now, I expected one of them to issue me an AARP card.

Donnelly scratched his greasy head and examined the scrapings trapped in his fingernails.

"Coulda been an accident. These things happen, you know."

"Just call the police."

"There's no need for the police, ma'am. We can do our own internal investigation."

Aha. Now I understood what was going on. Donnelly didn't want to call the cops because he didn't want any more negative publicity for the studio. Well, I didn't give a flying frisbee about the studio.

"Either you call the cops," I said. "Or I do."

"That won't be necessary."

I looked up and saw Detective Incorvia walking toward us.

"Detective Incorvia! Thank heavens you're here. Someone tried to drop a klieg light on my head."

"I'm glad they missed," he said. "Now calm down." He lead me over to Muffy's living-room sofa. "Can I get you something to drink? Some coffee?" He turned to the Security guys.

"Can one of you get us some coffee?"

"No," I said. "Get me the scotch."

"Scotch?"

"In the cookie jar."

He went to the kitchen and retrieved the scotch from the cookie jar.

"I see Muffy's been dipping into the sauce again," he said, smiling, as he handed me the bottle.

I took a healthy swig or three.

"Feeling better?"

I nodded.

"Okay, why don't you tell me exactly what happened."

And I did. In a giant rush of a run-on sentence, I told him everything. And I mean everything. I told him about the frog in my briefcase, and Bianca's hair ornament, about the Evian/gin bottle in Muffy's drawer, and how not a half hour after I'd been talking with Zach, a klieg light crashed on the kitchen table and almost killed me.

"Wow," he said, when I finally came up for air. "That's some story."

"Don't you see?" I said. "Everyone knows I've been asking questions about Quinn's murder. Someone obviously wants me to stop."

By now, a bunch of cops had arrived and were investigating the scene.

"Detective Incorvia!" one of them called from up on the catwalk.

"Yeah?"

"The wire's been cut."

"What did I tell you? This was no accident. Somebody wanted to kill me."

"It sure looks that way."

And suddenly I was terrified. I liked it a lot better when it could have been an accident.

Chapter Twenty

Detective Incorvia walked me to my car.

"Are you sure you'll be all right? I can have an officer drive you home."

"I'll be okay," I said, not meaning it. My heart was still bouncing around in my chest like a Ping-Pong ball. I could picture the headlines: *Freelance writer has heart attack on freeway. Medic who drags her mangled body out from behind the wheel says: "Never have I seen such ratty underwear."*

"Jaine? Are you sure you're okay?"

"I'm fine."

I was just opening the door to my Corolla when I thought to ask: "By the way, Detective, what were you doing here tonight?"

"I came to interview an employee. One of the cleaning crew." He took out his pad and consulted it. "Crista Alvarez. Apparently she saw someone sneak into the prop room a few minutes before the show started taping. At first Ms. Alvarez didn't want to get mixed up with the police. But then her husband convinced her to call us."

"My gosh. Who was it? Who did she see sneaking in to the prop room?"

"You're not going to like this," he said with a sigh.

"Why? Who was it?"

"Your friend Kandi."

"What the hell were you doing in the prop room?"

Kandi and I were in the living room of her high-tech, high-rise Westwood condo, where the living is easy and the rents are astronomical. I'd found her sprawled out on her spotless white sofa, watching a tape of *Miracle on 34th Street*, the treacly Natalie Wood movie about a kid who doesn't believe in Santa Claus.

"You know how many times I've seen this movie in the past week?" Kandi said. "Fifteen times."

"Fifteen?"

Kandi nodded. "It's so soothingly bland. It calms me down."

"Well," I said, pressing the mute button on the remote, "it's time to return to the Land of the Anxious. I repeat: What the hell were you doing in the prop room? Apparently a cleaning lady saw you sneaking in there before the show started."

Kandi sighed. "Getting closure."

She popped the cork on a bottle of wine. "Want some?"

I shook my head. Something told me I'd need to keep a clear head for this story.

"A couple of weeks ago we did a show called 'Spiffy Biff.' All about what happens when Uncle Biff meets a woman and tries to impress her by acting suave and debonair. In the show, Biff tries to be worldly and takes up smoking a pipe. After the show wrapped, I took the pipe from the prop room. I know it's insane, but I wanted it because it had touched Quinn's lips. I was so crazy in love with the guy. You know how that is."

Sad to say, I didn't.

"Of course, after I found out he'd been screwing around on me, I was furious. The last thing I wanted to look at was that damn pipe. Dr. Mellman told me to get rid of it. He said it would give me closure. So I brought it back to the prop room. I slipped in while Mr. Goldman was telling his knock-knock joke."

"Why didn't you tell me?"

"I was ashamed. I felt like such an idiot, stealing something because my lover's lips had touched it. Have you ever heard of anything so stupid?"

Actually I had. One of The Blob's proudest possessions was a laminated paper cocktail napkin that he swore Heather Locklear had used to blot her lipstick.

"So I guess Incorvia is convinced I'm the killer, huh?"

"No, not at all," I said, without much conviction.

"Oh, God, Jaine," Kandi said, slugging down some wine. "You've got to find the real killer."

I'd been planning to tell her about my near brush with death, but now I didn't have the heart to do it. She had enough to worry about.

I turned the sound back up on the television and kissed her on the forehead.

"Try to get some sleep, sweetie. I'm sure everything will work out."

She nodded numbly, and I walked out the door, *Miracle on 34th Street* droning softly in the background.

Poor Kandi. Not even Santa Claus could bail her out of this mess.

By the time I got back to my apartment, my terror—which had temporarily abated with the news of Kandi's prop room adventures—was back in full bloom. Someone had tried to kill me. Whoever it was might try again. And again. Until they finally got it right. A thought which sent me scurrying to my medicine cabinet in search of tranquilizers.

I rummaged through yellowing bottles of aspirin

and ancient moisturizers I'd bought while under the influence of a Clinique saleswoman/hypnotist. Finally I found what I was looking for: A bottle of Valium, left over from my divorce from The Blob. I save it for specially horrific occasions. (Like the time I saw myself in a three-way mirror in a pair of bicycle shorts.)

I opened the bottle and popped a pill in my mouth. I felt it working right away. The fact that I'd washed it down with a glass of chardonnay didn't hurt. I was feeling a lot calmer as I ran around the apartment checking the locks on my doors and windows.

Prozac, sensing how distressed I was and how much I needed her comforting presence, decided to take a nap.

"How can you sleep at a time like this?" I wailed. "Someone tried to kill me today."

She opened a baleful eye and shot me a look that said, *This never would have happened if you'd stayed home where you belong taking care of Me-Me-Me.*

Then she rolled over and went back to sleep, totally ignoring me. Much like The Blob used to do after sex.

I crept into bed with my chardonnay and a hot-water bottle and turned on the TV. Maybe, like Kandi, I could find a calming movie to watch. I zapped around, with no luck.

Why is it that whenever you're in desperate need of a good movie, all you ever find are those stultifyingly boring 50's gladiator flicks? Where actors like Tony Curtis and Ernest Borgnine run around in togas saying stuff like, "Caspius hath declareth war on the armies of Andronicus and Moronicus!"

I zapped my way past the gladiators, a monster movie, and the Three Stooges. I was about to give up and watch C-SPAN (always an effective sleep inducer) when I came across an old made-for-TV thriller about a psychopathic little boy who kills anyone who gets in his way. It was a shameless ripoff of *The Bad Seed*. Normally I would have zapped past. But there was something about this movie that made me stop: The little boy. I recognized him right away. It was Zach Levy-Taylor, the twelve-year-old version.

I'd know that bad acting anywhere.

There he was on my TV screen, killing his enemies at the slightest provocation. And you'll never guess what he killed them with: rat poison. That's right. The very same stuff that killed Quinn.

Suddenly Zach zoomed to the top of my suspect list. Was Quinn's murder a case of life imitating art? Had Zach bumped off his real-life enemy with the same poison he'd used to kill his fictional ones? Had he remembered his long-ago role and reenacted it on the *Muffy 'n Me* soundstage?

It all made sense to me. The kid had no imagination. I could easily picture him using an old script as a blueprint for murder.

And how did I know that Zach actually left the soundstage after our little chat tonight? Maybe he sneaked back in and climbed onto the catwalk while I was busy snooping in Muffy's bedroom. He knew I was investigating the murder. Maybe he was afraid of what I'd discover and decided to put an end to my questions with a lethal overhead light.

A million possibilities (all of them ghastly) buzzed in my brain. By now, I was utterly wired. No way could I relax. I tried C-SPAN and hot milk and reciting all of Elizabeth Taylor's husbands in alphabetical order. But nothing worked. Sleep was out of the question. I tossed and turned, and tossed some more.

It wasn't until about four A.M. when Prozac jumped in bed and curled up against my tummy that I was finally able to doze off.

I woke up the next morning bleary-eyed from lack of sleep. I'd left the TV on all night, and now an impossibly chirpy trio of pretty people with poufy hair were giggling their way through the morning news.

If you ask me, it should be a federal offense to be chirpy before nine A.M.

"And now," said a gorgeous Asian woman with poufy black hair, "let's hear the latest Tinseltown News from entertainment reporter Jim Freeman."

The camera cut to a cherubic guy with poufy red hair.

"Hey, kids!" the poufy redhead said. "Have I got news for you! More mayhem on the set of Miracle Studios' *Muffy 'n Me*. If you remember, last week cast member Quinn Kirkland was poisoned on stage while shooting an episode of the teen laffer. Now, less than a week later, the Morning News has learned that freelance writer Jaine Austen barely escaped death when a klieg light fell just inches from her head. Word on the street is—it was no accident. Which is why folks are now referring to *Muffy 'n Me* as *Murder 'n Me*."

His sidekicks chuckled appreciatively.

"With so much bad press, don't be surprised if this Saturday sitcom winds up in Cancellation City."

He then passed the baton to a poufy-haired weather guy, who said, "Jane Austen? Isn't she already dead?"

Gales of laughter from his fellow yuckmeisters. What a class act. Edward R. Murrow was probably rolling over in his grave. And I wasn't all that amused, either.

Just as I was hurling a few choice epithets at the TV, the phone rang. It was Kandi.

"I saw the news," she wailed. "Why didn't you tell me that you almost got killed last night?"

"I didn't want to worry you."

"What did they mean—it was no accident?"

"The electrical wires were cut."

"Oh, no," she moaned.

"Everybody knows I've been investigating Quinn's death. I guess somebody wants me to stop."

"You almost got killed, and it was all my fault."

"It's not your fault, Kandi. I think we can safely lay the blame on the person who cut the wires."

"If you hadn't been helping me out, this never would have happened."

She had a point there.

"You've got to promise me you'll stop. I couldn't live with myself if something happened to you."

I have to confess: There was a part of me that wanted to call it quits, that wanted to stay holed up with a rifle and a Doberman pinscher, and never again try anything riskier than anchovies on my pizza. At that moment, agoraphobia was looking like a mighty attractive lifestyle.

I was just about to say, *Maybe you're right. Maybe I should give up the investigation*, when I heard Kandi's doorbell ring in the background.

"Oh, gosh," she said. "I've got to go. The cops are here."

"The cops?"

"Yes, I have to go down to police headquarters."

My stomach sank. They really did think Kandi was the murderer.

"Are they arresting you?"

"No, they just want to ask me some more questions. But I'm not hanging up until you promise me you'll give up the investigation."

"Okay. I promise."

"You're lying, aren't you?"

"Yes," I admitted.

"Thank God!" she said. "For a minute, I was afraid you were going to do the sensible thing."

No such luck.

YOU'VE GOT MAIL!

TAMPATRIBUNE.COM

JEALOUS HUSBAND ASSAULTS SHOPPING
HOST ON LIVE TV; ACCUSES HIM OF HAVING
AFFAIR WITH HIS WIFE

TAMPA, FLORIDA—Home Shopping Club viewers
may have thought they were watching the World
Wrestling Federation last night when a jealous
husband stormed on stage and started pummeling
popular shopping channel host John Koskovalis.

Mr. Hank Austen of Tampa Villas claimed Mr.
Koskovalis was having an affair with his wife.

"I came to avenge my honor!" Mr. Austen said, shortly
before he was rushed off for emergency dental surgery
to replace three broken teeth.

TO: Jausten
FROM: Shoptillyoudrop
SUBJECT: Humiliated beyond belief!

You're not going to believe this, dear, but Daddy as-
saulted poor John Koskovalis on national TV. Accused
him of sleeping with me! Right in the middle of The
Jewelry Showcase! I swear, I'll never be able to show
my face in Tampa Villas again. What's gotten into him,
anyway?

TO: Shoptillyoudrop
FROM: Jausten
SUBJECT: The Bright Side

You've got to look on the bright side: At least Daddy loves you enough to be insanely jealous. Besides, he's always been overly excitable. Remember the time he was convinced the plumber stole our toilet plunger, and he filed a case in small claims court, and after he'd spent $900 for legal advice he found the plunger where he'd left it behind his galoshes in the basement?

TO: Jausten
FROM: Shoptillyoudrop

Yes, I do remember, and do you know how long it took before we could get another plumber to come out to the house? We were blacklisted for *months*. That was no picnic, let me tell you, right in the middle of melon season. Really, dear. I've had it up to my eyeballs with Daddy. I'm tired of putting up with his nonsense. I'm seriously thinking of moving back to California. How about us being roommates? Wouldn't that be fun?

TO: Shoptillyoudrop
FROM: Jausten
SUBJECT: The "D" Word

You're not thinking about the "D" word, are you?

TO: Jausten
FROM: Shoptillyoudrop

Honey, why on earth would I go on a diet at a time
like this? I'm way too upset to eat, anyway.

TO: Shoptillyoudrop
FROM: Jausten

Not "Diet"—"Divorce"!

TO: Jausten
FROM: Shoptillyoudrop

No, I haven't considered divorce. Murder, yes. But not
divorce.

PS. Speaking of murder, I heard on *Larry King* that
your friend Cookie is the Number One suspect in the
murder of Aidan Quinn! Poor thing!

TO: Shoptillyoudrop
FROM: Jausten

Actually, Mom, my friend's name is Kandi (not
Cookie), and the guy who got killed is Quinn
Kirkland (not Aidan Quinn).

And thank goodness you're not thinking of divorcing
Daddy. For a minute there you had me worried.

TO: Jausten
FROM: Shoptillyoudrop

Oh, no, honey. I wouldn't dream of going through the
bother and expense of a divorce. A legal separation is
good enough for me. So how about it, dear? Want to
be roomies? If I make my plane reservations today, I
can be there in two weeks.

Chapter Twenty-One

I drove to the studio in a state of shock. I didn't know what to be more upset over: the fact that someone had tried to kill me, or that my father had attacked a shopping host on national television.

Daddy had clearly flipped his wigwam. And now my mother was threatening to leave him—after forty-two years of marriage. True, they'd been driving each other crazy for forty-one and a half of those years, but I'd always believed that deep down they really loved each other. Had Daddy finally crossed the line and alienated Mom forever?

And what if Mom was serious about moving in with me? Just what I needed. A sixtysomething "roomie" with a closetful of sequinned T-shirts.

Oh, well. At least they hadn't heard about my close encounter with a klieg light.

I pulled up to the studio gates and saw that the place was swarming with news vans. Okay, so it wasn't exactly swarming. There were two measly vans, both of them from TV stations with viewerships in the double digits. A couple of bored reporters were standing around exchanging makeup tips.

"Hey," one of them said, catching sight of my car as

I stopped at the gate. "That might be her. The guard said she drove a crummy white Corolla."

They grabbed their mikes and raced to my side. "Are you Jaine Austen?" they asked, thrusting their mikes under my nose.

"Yes," I nodded warily.

"Any comment about what happened yesterday?"

"I don't know why he did it. My father's been under a lot of stress lately. I'm sure that with the right medication, he can return to a normal and productive life."

The reporters stared at me blankly, no doubt wondering what the hell I was talking about.

"Actually, I was referring to what happened last night here at the studio."

"Yeah," the other one said. "How does it feel to have come *thisclose* to getting killed?"

"Well—"

But Los Angeles was not about to get the inside skinny on my feelings. Because just then a bright red Miata came zooming up behind me.

"Look! It's Vanessa Dennis!"

I looked up into my rearview mirror, and sure enough, it was Vanessa. And sitting on the front seat beside her, looking awfully chummy, was Zach Levy-Taylor. If Zach killed Quinn to get rid of the competition, it sure seemed to be working.

I wondered if he was sleeping with Vanessa. Obviously the reporters were wondering the same thing because they dumped me like a hot potato and went racing to Vanessa's side.

Welcome to Hollywood. Where a near murder victim is never as newsworthy as a pretty girl with big tits.

Skippy, the ancient guard, stopped me at the gate.

"I heard what happened to you last night," he said, a

look of concern in his rheumy eyes. "How're you feeling?"

What a sweet guy. I was happy to know there was at least one compassionate person on the lot.

"I'm fine," I said. "Just fine."

"Listen, do you think maybe I could have your autograph?"

"My autograph? Why would you want my autograph?"

"In case anything . . . uh . . . happened to you, I could add it to my collection of murdered celebrities' autographs."

"What?"

"I've got 'em all," he boasted. "Sal Mineo, Bob Crane, Phil Hartman . . ."

I gave the old ghoul my autograph and drove onto the lot, pulling into my coveted spot next to the dumpster. Vanessa and Zach sped past me to the A-list parking area. I could see Zach's arm slung possessively around her shoulder. Why did I get the feeling that Vanessa would soon be reaching for another one of her bedside condoms?

I trekked over to the Writers' Building, picking up a stale danish from the commissary en route. I settled in at my desk, wondering if the white stuff on the danish was icing or mold. I threw caution to the winds and took a bite. It was icing. I only hoped that the little black things inside were raisins.

I hadn't been at my desk more than five minutes when Audrey summoned me to her office, looking particularly bloodless in a stark white suit and near-black lipstick. Grace Kelly meets Vampira. Stan was at his desk, reading the trades and sipping his morning cup of gin.

"We heard about what happened last night," Audrey said.

And believe it or not, she actually looked upset. Who knew? Maybe she did have a warm and cuddly side, after all.

"And I want you to know that . . ." She paused dramatically.

Extra credit for those of you who guess how she finished that sentence:

A) "Stan and I are thrilled with the work you've been doing."

B) "We feel so bad that you almost got your skull bashed in, we're going to cut you a generous check for pain and suffering."

C) "We'd like you to come on board as a permanent staff member."

Those of you who guessed None of the Above, go to the head of the class.

"I just want you to know," she said, tapping her nails on her desk in an angry staccato, "that I never *ever* want you bothering the actors again."

So much for warm and cuddly.

"Several people have told me you've been prying into their lives with some pretty invasive questions."

I wondered who'd squealed on me. Probably Zach. What a crybaby.

"I'd appreciate it if you'd leave any and all detective work to the police. Is that understood?"

"Yes, Sarge."

Okay, so I didn't really call her Sarge. I said I understood, and promised never to bother her precious actors again. A promise which I intended to break at the earliest possible opportunity.

At that moment Bianca poked her head in the door.

"*Entertainment Tonight* is waiting for you and Stan down on the stage."

Audrey nodded.

"Damage control," she said to me, in a way that implied that I was somehow responsible for the damage.

She got up and straightened her suit, which, of course, needed no straightening. Then she turned to Stan.

"C'mon, Stan," she said, brushing the lint off his sweatshirt. "Time to meet the press. And remember. Let me do the talking."

Then she sniffed his breath.

"Jesus, Stan. There's enough gin on your breath to make a martini. Whatever you do," she said, herding him out the door, "don't breathe on Mary Hart."

Chapter Twenty-Two

Alone in Stan and Audrey's office, I took a look around. Compared to our office, it was the Taj Mahal. Of course, compared to our office, a toolshed was the Taj Mahal.

This was the moment I'd been waiting for. With Stan and Audrey gone, I could easily slip Lance's treatment on Audrey's desk.

Well, maybe not so easily, after all. I'd forgotten about Bianca.

There she was, at her post in the reception area, guarding the inner sanctum like a bitchy gargoyle. She'd never let me back in without a probing inquisition. I had to think of some way to get rid of her.

"Hey, Bianca," I said, strolling over to her desk.

She didn't bother to look up from her Cosmo Quiz.

"You'll never guess who's on the lot today."

"Who?" she said, still not bothering to look up.

"Brad Pitt."

"Get outta here!"

At last she made eye contact.

"I heard he's shooting a public service spot over at the haunted house set."

"I love Brad Pitt," she sighed. "I absolutely adore him."

"Why don't you go over and watch them shoot?"

"Are you kidding? Audrey would kill me if I left the phones."

"Don't sweat it. I'll answer the phones for you."

"Would you?" she asked.

"Sure. It's no problem."

"Gee, thanks," she said, smiling a brittle smile. (Hey, she wasn't used to being nice; it was the best she could do.)

And she sped out of there faster than a BMW in a hospital zone.

The minute she was gone, I retrieved Lance's treatment from my briefcase. I quickly buried it in a pile of scripts on Audrey's desk and breathed a sigh of relief. Thank goodness I'd gotten that over with. Now I could say in all honesty, when Lance next asked me, that I'd given his damn shoe saga to Audrey.

I plopped myself down in Audrey's swivel chair and spun around. What luxury to sit on a chair that didn't need fumigating. And then, before I knew it, I was peeking in her desk drawers. I couldn't help myself. This snooping thing can be very addictive.

Audrey's desk was a gleaming teak affair, a far cry from my wormy woodpile. The insides of her drawers were spotless, as opposed to mine, which were coated with petrified gum and inkstains from the Punic Wars. Her pens were lined up neatly in a pen compartment, along with some lipsticks and an eyelash curler. Her file drawers yielded little of interest. Just some old scripts and a Neiman Marcus catalogue. Too bad. I was hoping for something a lot more incriminating.

I wandered over to Stan's desk, where I found an impressive supply of gin bottles stashed in his file drawer. The rest of his drawers were amazingly empty for a man supposedly running a television show. All I found was a bottle of Maalox and a brochure for a vacation condominium in Palm Springs.

No rat poison in sight.

I was just about to call it quits when I looked over at Audrey's desk and noticed her datebook. It was hand-tooled leather, buttery soft, her initials discreetly embossed in the corner.

I debated the ethics of invading Audrey's private records for a second or two, then opened the book. Every entry was written in black ink, printed carefully in attractive block letters. Quelle neatnik. The woman probably color-coded her bras.

I glanced through the entries, taking in Audrey's busy schedule of network meetings, business lunches, manicures and hair colorist appointments. Aha, so that perfect blond hair of hers came from a bottle. Very gratifying.

Every once in a while, I'd see an entry simply marked "Q." If the "Q" stood for Quinn, and I strongly suspected it did, it looked like Audrey had been meeting him at least once a week.

On a hunch, I checked the entry for the day of the murder. There, between "network meeting" and "dinner—Spago," was another "Q." Did that mean she planned to meet Quinn that day? Did she want to have it out with him once and for all? Or was she beyond meetings? Had she already made up her mind? Had she decided not to meet him, but to murder him instead?

My thoughts were interrupted by the sound of Bianca breathing fire. I looked up and saw her glowering in the doorway.

"Brad Pitt's not shooting a commercial on the lot," she hissed.

"Oh?" I said, surreptitiously closing Audrey's datebook. "Somebody told me he was."

"And what the hell are you doing in here?" she said, narrowing her already beady eyes.

"Uh . . . Audrey called and asked me to bring her something from her desk."

"Bullshit." She smiled slyly. "You were snooping. And I'm going to tell Audrey."

"You do," I said, "and I'll tell the cops about the deal you made with Danny to give each other alibis."

It was a gamble, but I had to take it.

It worked. Her face went white with fear.

"How did you know about that?"

"It doesn't matter how I know. I just know, that's all."

I walked over to her, trying my best to look tough.

"You keep your mouth shut," I said, "or I'll call the cops. I mean it."

She nodded numbly.

Then I strode back into my office, not missing a beat.

Gosh, I was getting good at this.

Stan and Audrey were still down on stage chatting it up with *Entertainment Tonight* when Kandi came back from the cops.

"How'd it go?" I asked, as she trudged into the office.

"They warned me not to leave the country."

She plopped on the sofa, limp with defeat.

"I should've gone to dental hygienist school like my mother wanted me to. I should have stayed in New York and married Sandy Needleman the accountant. But no, I had to be a big-deal comedy writer. I had to have an affair with an ac-tor. And I had to be the idiot who volunteered to get those damn donuts."

She shook her head, dazed, as if unable to believe the shit that was hitting her fan.

"Oh, God," she moaned. "Any day now I'm going to be sharing a jail cell with a woman named Big Earl."

"Kandi, honey. Listen to me. They can't arrest you just because someone happened to see you go into the prop room. It proves nothing."

"Do you know how many innocent people are jailed

each year for crimes they didn't commit? Hundreds, probably thousands."

"Kandi, you've got to stop thinking such negative thoughts."

"That's what Dr. Mellman says." She took out a small book from her purse.

"What's that?" I asked.

"A book of affirmations. I'm supposed to say a new one each day." She opened the book and read one aloud: *I trust the process of life. I am safe. I am free.*

"Yeah, right," she said, tossing the book aside. "Free to remain silent because anything I say can and will be held against me."

"Look," I said, trying desperately to lift her spirits, "we'll go to Dale's party tonight. We'll mellow out, have some laughs, some free hors d'oeuvres. Who knows? Maybe Melanie and Antonio and Julia and Brad will be there."

"I can't go to Dale's party."

"Why not?"

"Tonight's my night at the soup kitchen."

"The soup kitchen?"

"I made a deal with God. If She gets me out of this mess, I promised to lead a worthy life. I promised not to obsess about trivial stuff like men and cellulite, and to devote my energies to noble causes. So I signed up to feed the homeless one night a week. And tonight's my night."

"That's great," I said, somewhat dubiously. Somehow I just couldn't picture Kandi in a soup kitchen. I only hoped she wouldn't wind up dating one of the residents. But I smiled encouragingly, hoping that her time spent there would help put her own problems in perspective.

"Well, I'm going to the party," I said. "I want to nose around and ask some more questions."

"Are you sure you want to keep doing this, Jaine? After what happened last night?"

"I'm sure." In spite of Audrey's gag order, I was determined not to give up on the case.

"Oh, Jaine! I don't know what I'd do without you."

Kandi's eyes filled with tears, and she threw her arms around me. We sat hugging each other for at least five minutes.

Good practice, Kandi said, for when she moved in with Big Earl.

Chapter
Twenty-Three

I was soaking in the tub, with my hair in a turban and a pore strip on my nose, writing out my list of suspects. I was determined to clarify my thoughts (and my blackheads) before Dale's party. I had just managed to balance a legal pad on my bath-oily thighs when the phone rang. I let the machine get it.

"Hi, Jaine. It's me, Lance. Hope you're enjoying your bath. I can hear you splashing around in there."

Good heavens. With neighbors like Lance, why bother with walls?

"I was just about to head out, but I thought I'd call and find out how things are going with Audrey. Did she say anything about my treatment?"

"No, Lance," I called out. "Not yet."

"Oh. Too bad. Let me know when she does, okay?"

And then he hung up.

I don't mind admitting I was a bit shaken. If Lance could hear me splashing around in the tub, I hated to think what else he could hear in my bathroom. Oh, well. No time to worry about that now. Not with a murder waiting to be solved.

I went back to my list of suspects, scribbling away on the damp legal pad. And then, just when I was almost through, the damn thing fell into the water. I fished it out, and blew away the bubbles. It was still faintly legible, so if you want to read it, here it is:

My Suspects
by Jaine Austen

Audrey Miller. Ice Queen and Scorned Lover. Threatened to "get rid of" Quinn. Very possible that she did. Easy enough to slip into the prop room on her way back from her network meeting and sprinkle some rat poison on a box of donuts.

Stan Miller. Ineffectual alcoholic, specializing in gin consumption. Knew that Audrey was sleeping with Quinn. Possibly sleeping with Vanessa himself? Either way, he'd been cuckolded by Quinn. Could he have poisoned him in a jealous rage? More important, could he have stayed sober long enough to do it?

Vanessa Dennis. Did Quinn break her young heart? Did she get even with a deadly donut? Claims she was in her trailer while the prop room was left unattended, but she also claims her boobs are her own. So much for her credibility.

Zach Levy-Taylor. Obviously loathed Quinn, threatened to kill him in front of a stageful of people. Did he reenact his murderous TV movie role and bump off his enemy? And then, scared that I would discover the truth, did he snip the wires on the overhead light?

*Dale Burton. Overheard telling his agent
he was going to "do something" to save his
job. Was that "something" murder?*

*Vanessa's mom. Mousy on the outside. The
Terminator on the inside? Found out Quinn
was boffing her daughter and cooked up a
way to get rid of him?*

*Bianca. Frustrated secretary and irritat-
ing bitch. Probably boffing Quinn. Lied to
the cops about her whereabouts the night
of the murder. My choice for Woman I'd
Most Like to See Turn Out to be the Murderer.*

Danny, the Production Ass—

No, that wasn't an editorial comment. That was when
the list fell in the water. After I blew it dry with my hair
dryer, I read it over. Sad to say, no startling insights occurred. I was just as confused as when I started out. I
promised myself I'd study it in excruciating detail the
minute I got back from Dale's party.

In the meanwhile, though, I had to get dressed. I
threw on a pair of black slacks and a black turtleneck
sweater. I was going for the unobtrusive look. My goal
was to blend in with the scenery, so people would forget I was there and talk openly. Leaving my hair and
makeup for last, I headed off to feed Prozac.

"Dinner time," I called out gaily.

Prozac, who was hard at work trying to shed as much
fur as possible on the living room sofa, decided to ignore me.

I reached into my purse and took out a can of crabmeat I'd bought on my way home from the studio.

"Look, honey," I said, waving the can in front of her. "Look what Mommy bought you for dinner! A seven-dollar can of crabmeat!"

She sniffed at it dismissively as if to say, *What, no caviar?*

"C'mon, sweetpea," I said, heading back to the kitchen. "It's delicious."

I guess she must have decided she was hungry, because she started trotting after me. The minute I reached for the can opener, she knew food was in the offing, and she began doing what she always does when food is in the offing: yowling and clinging to my ankles, in the mistaken belief that tripping me will somehow get the food on her plate faster.

I was just starting to open the crabmeat when tragedy struck. The can opener broke.

Now Prozac was yowling louder than ever, demanding to be fed. The poor thing was ravenous. After all, it had probably been a whole twenty minutes since she'd last snacked on her bowl of dry cat food.

"Just a minute," I said, "Mommy's can opener broke. Mommy'll have to find you something else to eat."

I hurried to see what I had in the refrigerator. I would have given her leftovers, but there *were* no leftovers. There are never any leftovers in my refrigerator, because in order to get leftovers, you actually have to cook. There was nothing in my refrigerator except for a half a bottle of chardonnay and that jar of garlic-stuffed olives.

By now, Prozac was in high hysteria mode. Think Janet Leigh in the shower scene in *Psycho*.

"Don't panic," I said, grabbing my keys. "Mommy will just run over to the hardware store and buy another can opener. I'll be right back, I promise."

I ran down to Olympic Boulevard and then two blocks east to Beverly Hardware, the world's most expensive hardware store, where you need a co-signer to buy a hammer.

I dashed in, prepared to fork over whatever they were overcharging for a simple can opener. I was rummaging around the kitchen gadget section, searching for a can opener that cost less than a Porsche, when I heard the clerk say: "Will that be all, Mr. Miller?"

Now I'm sure there are scads of Millers in the city of Los Angeles. Any one of whom could have been in Beverly Hardware that night. I don't know why I thought that this one might be Stan. But I did. I vaguely remembered Kandi telling me that he and Audrey lived somewhere in Beverly Hills.

I tiptoed over to the end of the aisle and—hiding behind a display of Roach Motels—peered out at the checkout counter.

Sure enough, it was Stan.

"So, Mr. Miller," the clerk was saying, "how did that poison work out for you?"

Stan paled. "Poison?" he said, practically choking on the word.

"The rat poison you bought last week. Did it get rid of your rats?"

Stan stood there, blinking, struggling to make his mouth work.

"Uh . . .yes," he finally managed to mumble. "It worked fine."

And with that, he grabbed his package and hurried out the door.

"Can I help you miss?"

I looked over and saw the clerk staring at me. It wasn't every day he found a customer hiding out at the Roach Motels.

I held up one of the "motels."

"Does the room come with cable TV?" I asked, going for a joke.

"Huh?" he replied, going for the security alarm. The guy clearly had me pegged for a loony. And then I glanced up at the overhead security mirror and saw that I still had that damn pore strip on my nose! No wonder he was so spooked.

I quickly grabbed a twenty-dollar can opener and paid for it before he could put in a call to the Cedars Sinai psychiatric ward.

I made my way back home in a daze, still shocked at what I had overheard. So Stan had bought rat poison. Of course, it was possible he actually bought it to kill rats. Rats are a common problem in Los Angeles. So maybe it was a perfectly innocent purchase.

And if you believe that, I've got a comedy about a bunch of shoe salesmen I'd like to sell you.

Chapter
Twenty-Four

The first thing I did when I got home was call Detective Incorvia. The desk sergeant said he wasn't in, that he was at a UCLA screenwriting course. I left a message telling him to call me as soon as possible and hung up, secure in the knowledge that the city was safe from poor story structure.

Then I fed Prozac and wrenched that ridiculous pore strip off my nose. Which wasn't easy. The damn thing had hardened to the consistency of cement. I practically needed a hacksaw to get it off. Not only did it remove all my blackheads; as an added bonus, it also yanked off a healthy layer of skin. Which left my nose a lovely shade of Rudolph Reindeer Red.

I headed out to the party, my nose glowing and my brain on overdrive. I couldn't stop thinking about the bombshell in the hardware store. So Stan had bought rat poison the week before the murder. It sure made him the leading contender in the Murder Suspect Sweepstakes. And yet, it was hard to picture Stan as a cold-blooded killer. The only thing he seemed capable of killing were my jokes.

I would've thought for sure that Audrey was the murderer in that family. And maybe she was. It was very possible that Stan was just following her orders when he bought the rat poison, never dreaming that the rat she intended to use it on was Quinn Kirkland.

Or maybe they were in it together, a husband and wife crime. The family that slays together, stays together—that sort of thing.

I made my way over the Sepulveda Pass to the San Fernando Valley and found Dale's house nestled in a leafy cul de sac on the wrong side of Ventura Boulevard. Ventura is one of those L.A. streets that separate the rich from the middle class. The big bucks settle south of the boulevard; the regular Joes go north. And Dale's place was two blocks north of Ventura, just up the street from one of my favorite culinary establishments, The House of Wieners.

It was a sprawling ranch house, with lots of flag-stones and wind chimes, very Casa Suburbia. I knew I was in trouble when I rang the doorbell and it played the theme from *The Godfather.*

A sullen teenager in hip-hugger jeans and a midriff as tight as a trampoline answered the door. I assumed she was Dale's daughter.

"You with the show?" she asked.

"Yes, I'm Jaine—"

"C'mon in," she interrupted, not giving a damn who I was. She ushered me into a large woodsy living room, where a fire sputtered in an oversized stone fireplace. Hardly anyone was there. Just a handful of people. Most of them were below-the-line crew members, burly guys with big guts—the Beer Belly Brigade. Dale was no-where in sight.

"Where's your dad?" I asked Miss Hip-hugger.

"How should I know?" She shrugged. "Haven't seen him in twenty years."

"So Dale's not your father?"

She laughed, a bitter laugh. "Hell, no. He's my hus-band."

"Gee, I'm so sorry—"

"Me, too, honey."

In the shadowy foyer, she'd looked like a teenager. Now, upon closer inspection, I could see she was older. Not much older. Mid-twenties, tops. Like Vanessa, she had a prematurely hardened look. By the time she hit thirty, she'd be tougher than leather.

Now I knew why Dale was so desperate to keep his job. The minute he was out of work, I felt certain, his young bride would be gone with the wind chimes.

"Help yourself to some chow," she said, pointing to a buffet table laden with food. Uniformed waiters stood in a bored cluster behind the table. "I told Dale not to spring for a caterer. We could've ordered a platter from Jerry's Deli. But no, he had to impress Stan and Audrey. Who, incidentally, didn't even bother to show up."

"That's too bad," I said.

"Nobody important showed," she sighed, clearly pegging me as one of the unimportant. "Except for the old fart—he stopped by."

"The old fart?"

"The Brit with the snooty accent."

"You mean Wells Dumont?"

"Yeah. He put in a token appearance. Left about five minutes ago. Bored everybody senseless with a story about the time he gave a command performance of *Norman Lear* for Queen Elizabeth."

"*Norman Lear*? Don't you mean *King Lear*?"

"Whatever. Say, what happened to your nose? It's all red. You get a peel?"

"Something like that."

"Well, if you need to use the can, it's down that way. There's some concealer in the medicine cabinet."

She pointed vaguely down the hall, and yawned.

"I've had it with this fiasco. I'm going to bed."

"Nice talking to you," I called after her as she clomped away on impossibly high heels.

She was right, of course. The party was a major fiasco. Except for Dale, none of my prime suspects had shown up. And even Dale's whereabouts were a mystery. Oh, well, I thought, glancing at the buffet. At least there was food.

It was then that I noticed Bianca, huddled with Danny on a love seat near the window. They were deep in discussion, Bianca talking in an angry whisper.

"Okay," Danny finally said, loud enough for me to hear. "I won't say anything to anybody. I promise."

Then Bianca looked over and saw me. Her face went white.

"C'mon," she said, "let's get out of here."

She pulled Danny up from the sofa.

"But I haven't finished my drink."

"Yes, you have." She grabbed his drink out of his hand and slammed it down on a nearby coffee table.

The next thing I knew they were out the door.

No doubt about it: I'd scared the stuffing out of Bianca. And it felt great.

I headed over to the buffet table, where several stunning actor/waiters were standing around grousing.

"This was supposed to be an A-list party," I heard one of them say as I helped myself to some gorgeous shrimp.

"Yeah, I was told Antonio Banderas was coming."

"And Cameron Diaz."

"There's nobody here but drones."

They didn't even bother to lower their voices.

"Hi, there," I said to the beautiful young man behind the omelette cooker. "You think you could make an omelette for one of us drones?"

He sighed petulantly.

"Whaddaya want in it?"

"Just tomatoes. And maybe some onions. And a smidgeon of ham."

Reluctantly, he tossed together a burnt-on-the-bottom omelette and hurled it on a plate. I added some fresh fruit and just the weensiest mound of scalloped potatoes.

Then I wandered over to the Beer Belly Brigade, who were in the middle of a scintillating discussion about Athlete's Foot.

"I knew a guy who had it so bad," one of them said, "he had to have his big toe amputated."

"No shit."

"Hi," I said.

They looked up at me blankly.

"I'm Jaine Austen."

"Oh, yeah. From accounting, right?"

"No, I'm one of the writers."

"You the one that almost got killed?"

"That's me."

"Wow. You okay?"

"Sure. I'm fine."

"Your nose looks sorta funny."

"It's nothing. Just a little cosmetic mishap."

I smiled weakly and walked away. I suppose I should've pumped them for information about the murder, but something about them (their double digit IQs, perhaps) told me I wasn't going to learn anything useful.

Instead, I strolled over to the fireplace and glanced up at the framed photos on the mantel. At first I thought they were family pictures. But then I saw they were 8x10 glossies of famous actors: Antonio, Melanie, Cameron, Brad, Gwyneth. All autographed. Just like at a dry cleaner's. But dry cleaners usually know their customers. I had a sneaky suspicion Dale had bought these pictures at one of those movie memorabilia shops on Hollywood Boulevard.

By now I'd snarfed down my omelette and my fruit and my potatoes and my shrimp. If only those damn actor/waiters weren't hovering by the buffet table, I could nab some more shrimp to bring home for Prozac.

I checked out the desserts and in an impressive burst of willpower, I walked right by them.

Okay, so I made a pitstop at the cookie tray and had a tiny chocolate brownie.

Okay, so it wasn't so tiny and I had two.

Wiping the brownie crumbs from my lips, I started down the hallway in search of the bathroom. I wanted to check on my nose, and maybe try some of that concealer Dale's wife had told me about.

There were a several doors along the hallway. I had no idea which one was the bathroom. I certainly didn't want to barge in on Mrs. Dale polishing her toenails or phoning her lover or doing whatever it was she normally did before she went to bed.

I stopped at a door and knocked. No answer. I opened it, and gasped in horror.

It turns out it wasn't the bathroom, but a closet—filled with row after row of disembodied heads! Good heavens. This was straight out of *Nightmare on Elm Street*. Dale was obviously a mass murderer who decapitated his victims and saved their heads as grisly souvenirs!

And then, to my profound relief, I realized they weren't human heads, but wig holders. Each Styrofoam head sported a different wig. And every one of them looked just like Dale's boyish mop. It was the exact same style, only in different lengths. Hadn't I read about something like this before? Where a Hollywood producer kept thirty different wigs, one for each day of the month, each one slightly longer than the next? So people would think his hair was growing, and no one would ever guess that he was as bald as an eagle?

Poor Dale. Everything about him was just so damn pathetic.

At this point, I didn't care about my nose; all I wanted was something to calm me down. That closetful of disembodied heads had given me quite a scare. I hurried back to the living room where I snagged a glass of champagne. (And, if you must know, another brownie.)

The Beer Belly Brigade were still discussing amputations ("I knew a guy once who had his earlobe bit off!"), so I decided to go outside and get a breath of fresh air.

I walked out a sliding glass door onto a stark concrete patio. Dale was out there, alone in the moonlight. He sat on a deck chair, drinking what looked like a tumbler of scotch and tossing cheese puffs into his thimble-sized swimming pool.

He looked up at the sound of my footsteps. His normally clean-cut features were haggard; his sharp jawline was blurry with booze.

"Oh," he said, clearly disappointed that it was only me. "Hi, Judy."

"Actually, it's Jaine."

"Whatever."

He threw another cheese puff into the pool. Was it my imagination, or was his boyish head of hair slightly askew on his scalp?

"Look," he said, pointing to the cheese puffs. "They float."

"Is that so?" I smiled weakly.

"C'mere, June. Sit down." He patted the chair next to him. "At least somebody from the writing staff showed up."

Gingerly, I took a seat, wishing I'd asked for a double on the champagne.

"I hate them all," he said, grabbing another handful of cheese puffs and tossing them into the water. "The writers. The actors. Everybody."

The cheese puffs shimmered on the surface of the brightly lit pool like tiny white turds.

"Vanessa," he sneered, gulping some scotch. "The little slut couldn't act her way out of a paper bag. And Zach. You know what I call him? The oak."

"The oak?"

"The most wooden actor I've ever seen. Just stands on stage looking pretty. And Wells. What a bore. If I hear one more story about Larry Olivier, I'm going to puke."

And indeed he looked as if he might puke any minute. I tucked my legs under my chair, just in case.

"But at least Wells had the decency to put in an appearance tonight. Which is more than I can say for Audrey and Stan."

Dale tossed some more cheese puffs into the pool. By now it was a regular cheese puff regatta in there.

"What a pair," he sighed. "I knew them back when they were nobodies. When Audrey was just a production assistant, sleeping her way to the middle. And Stan was a below-the-line slob, working as a gaffer."

"A gaffer?" I'd seen the title a million times on movie credits and never knew what the heck it was. "What's that?"

"A lighting electrician."

It's a good thing I'd already finished my brownie. Otherwise it would've gone flying right out of my mouth. If Stan had been a lighting electrician, then he could have easily rigged the overhead light that almost killed me.

"Stan used to work with lights?"

"Yeah. He was gaffer on a bunch of shows. In fact, I think he once worked on a show with Wells, back when Wells was starring in some cockamamie Shakespearean sitcom. What was the name of that thing?"

He scratched his head, trying to remember.

"Oh, yeah," he said. "Now I remember. *That Darn Hamlet.*"

This time, there was no doubt about it. His boyish head of hair was definitely listing to the left.

"What an idiotic idea." By now he was slurring his

words pretty badly. "Who the hell wants to see a comedy about Hamlet? It got cancelled after three episodes."

"Isn't that awfully soon for a show to be cancelled?"

"The ratings stunk. Besides, I think there was some kind of accident on the set."

"An accident? What kind of accident?"

"I'm not sure. All I remember is somebody got hurt real bad. So the network pulled the plug."

"Was it a lighting accident?"

But I wasn't about to find out. Because just then Dale took a final slug of his scotch and passed out.

I grabbed the rest of the cheese puffs and got the hell out of there.

Back in my Corolla, I called Kandi on my cell phone. Luckily, she was home from her gala night at the Salvation Army and was able to give me Wells's phone number. I wanted to see him right away, so I could find out more about that accident on the set of *That Darn Hamlet*.

"How was the soup kitchen?" I asked.

"Fab," she sighed. "Some toothless guy with lint in his beard asked me out for Saturday night. I would've said yes, if it hadn't been for the swastika tattooed on his forehead."

"And they say there are no good men left in L.A."

"So what about you?" Kandi asked. "How was the party?"

"A ghost town. Dale's practically suicidal."

"Tell him to join the club."

"Cheer up, kiddo. I've got good news. I think I may know who killed Quinn."

"Who?" she squealed.

"Stan. Or, more likely, Stan acting on Audrey's orders."

"How do you know?"

I told her about what I'd seen at the hardware store.

"So Stan bought rat poison! Then he must be the killer. Oh, thank God. You've solved the case. Now this whole awful mess will be over."

"Don't break out the champagne yet. Just because he bought the poison doesn't mean he necessarily used it to kill Quinn. I think the cops need more evidence than that."

"But still, it's pretty damn incriminating. Did you tell Incorvia?"

"I left a message. He was out at a screenwriting class."

"Jeez," Kandi groaned. "Our tax dollars at work."

"Look, I've got to go. Talk to you later."

"Thanks, Jaine," she said, with a catch in her voice. "I knew you'd come through for me."

I hung up, praying that I would.

Chapter
Twenty-Five

I drove over to Wells's modest ivy-covered cottage in Santa Monica. And I do mean modest. The house hadn't seen a coat of paint in at least thirty years.

Wells answered the door in—I kid you not—a smoking jacket. With a silk ascot tied around his neck. I thought I'd died and been reincarnated in a Noel Coward play.

"Jaine, dear," he said, "how lovely to see you. Come in."

He led me into his living room. I'd thought Dale's house was a tad on the shabby side. But this place made Dale's look like something out of *Architectural Digest*. In spite of the dim lighting, I could see water stains on the ceiling and holes in the carpeting. I don't know what Wells was doing with his weekly paycheck, but it certainly wasn't earmarked for home improvements. Those water stains were older than I was.

"What can I get you to drink?" he asked, once I was settled on a rumpsprung sofa.

"Nothing, thank you. I'm fine."

The sofa was one of those low-slung Danish Modern models, so popular in the fifties. Now, a half a century later, with most of its padding shot to hell, it was practically grazing the floor. I sat doubled over, my knees jutting into my chest. I'd probably need a crane to haul myself out of it.

"So how can I help you, my dear? You said on the phone it was a matter of utmost importance."

"I wanted to know about the accident on the set of *That Darn Hamlet*."

"Ah. The Hamlet sitcom. The network said Americans weren't ready for an Elizabethan sitcom. Sadly, they were right. But I still feel certain that if they'd only given us a chance, we would've eventually found our audience."

He shook his head, bemoaning his—and America's—loss. Then, finally, he remembered I'd asked him a question.

"So, what was it you wanted to know?"

"The accident on the show, did it have anything to do with a falling light?"

"Why, yes. It hadn't occurred to me until now, but it was just like what happened to you the other day. Which reminds me—how are you feeling, my dear?"

"Just fine."

"Are you sure? I know an excellent podiatrist if you need one."

"No, really. I'm okay. Tell me more about the accident."

"There's not much to tell. An overhead light fell. It just missed one of the crew members."

"Did they ever find out if it was really an accident? Were the wires frayed, or did someone cut them?"

His silvery brows wrinkled in thought. "I'm afraid I don't remember. But I think I've got a clipping about it in my scrapbook. I'll go get it."

He walked out of the room, limping slightly. His feet were probably hurting again. At that moment I realized how much effort it must have taken for him to show up at work every day.

I heard him rattling around in the hall closet.

"Thanks so much for helping me out like this," I called out.

"My pleasure, my dear," he said, shuffling back into the room with a huge old-fashioned ribbon-bound scrapbook. As he set it down on the coffee table, dust flew from its pages.

He flipped through the pages until he found what he was looking for.

"Here it is," Wells said, pointing to a faded clipping. *Near Fatal Accident on Sitcom Set.*

The article told how an overhead light fell on the set of *That Darn Hamlet*, nearly missing one of the cameramen. Police said in all likelihood it was an accident, but they could not rule out the possibility of foul play. No arrests were made.

They couldn't rule out foul play. Which meant maybe there *had* been foul play. And maybe Stan was the foul player.

"As long as it's out," Wells said, "may I show you my scrapbook?"

Oh, God, no. The last thing I wanted to do was look at his humungous scrapbook. Really, I'd seen smaller carry-on luggage. But he smiled at me so hopefully, I just couldn't say no.

"Sounds great," I said.

And for the next hour I sat by his side, my knees stabbing my chest, looking at the highlights of Wells Dumont's theatrical career. I saw a picture of him at his first job, working as an acrobat in the circus. ("Just like Cary Grant started out," he beamed.) I saw him working as a magician ("Dumont the Great"), as a clown (Dumont the Silly), and as a spear carrier in an opera.

"Here's my very first review," Wells said, pointing to a yellowed clipping. *"Wells Dumont as The Irate Husband lent a comic touch to the proceedings."*

I waded through pictures of Wells as Hamlet, Othello,

Macbeth, and Felix Unger in a British production of
The Odd Couple.

Somewhere between Macbeth and Felix, I came
across a publicity photo of a delicate young woman
dressed in Elizabethan garb.

"That was my wife, Jessica."

"How beautiful she was."

"It was taken in Stratford-upon-Avon. That's where
we met, on a production of *Macbeth*. Ever since then,
Macbeth has been my favorite play."

He stared at the picture of the lovely young woman,
her large eyes gazing into the distance. Then he sighed
and turned the page.

We plowed our way through what seemed like a million more pictures and press clippings. Finally, we came
to the last page. On it was pasted an obituary: *Jessica
Dumont, British Stage Actress, Dead at 63*.

The middle-aged woman smiling out from her obituary picture was every bit as lovely as she had been in
her twenties.

"How sad that she died so young," I said. "How did
it happen?"

"Heart attack." Wells brushed an imaginary speck of
dust from his wife's picture.

"She'd gone to lunch with friends. They ate at a restaurant in Malibu, next to some brush area. Somehow
a snake had gotten into her car. She was driving back
home and discovered it. That's what the doctors said
probably gave her the heart attack."

His eyes misted over.

"It's just not the same without her," he said, struggling to hold back the tears.

Then he shut the scrapbook abruptly.

"Well," he said, forcing a smile. "I've kept you here
way too long, my dear. I'm so glad you stopped by."

"Me, too," I said. And, strangely enough, I meant it.
They say that when you get old, you find yourself

telling your life story over and over again. I don't know why. Maybe to make sense of your days on earth before they slip away. Wells had obviously needed someone to share his memories with. And, in the end, I was happy to do it.

Somehow I managed to dredge myself out of the sofa. Wells walked me to the door and waved good-bye.

He stood there in the doorway, a frail old man in a stained smoking jacket, with nothing left from his glory days except his fabulous head of hair.

As I headed down the path to the Corolla, I wondered why so many people struggle so hard to get into show business. So far, all I'd seen behind the cameras was grief and heartbreak.

It was after eleven when I got home. Which meant all the good parking spots were taken. And the bad ones, too. That's one of the negatives of living in a quaint Beverly Hills duplex: Lots of character, but no garage.

Usually I manage to find a spot somewhere on the street, but that night I was stuck parking two blocks away.

I got out of the Corolla and headed back to my apartment, walking briskly, my head held high, to let any potential muggers/rapists/Avon salesladies know that I was one tough cookie.

True, Beverly Hills isn't exactly a hotbed of crime. But I never like walking alone after dark. And I was especially uneasy, knowing that just the other day someone had tried to kill me. What if that same person was lurking behind a tree ready to pounce? What if he/she'd been following me all night just waiting for his/her chance to do me in? If I planned on being a detective, I chided myself, I really had to start looking for bad guys tailing me in my rearview mirror.

By now, convinced that a hardened killer was stalking me, I abandoned my head-held-high-tough-girl pose and broke into a scaredy-cat trot.

As I panted down the street, I told myself I was being silly. No one was going to come lurching out from behind a tree. But as luck would have it, just as I reached my duplex, someone *did* come lurching out from behind a tree. A short guy in a sweatsuit. I couldn't see him clearly in the dark, but it looked an awful lot like Stan.

"Jaine? Is that you?"

"Don't come any closer," I said, my voice squeaky with fear. "I've got a can of mace."

Frantically I rummaged through my purse. Indeed I did have a can of mace. I'd bought it years ago at a YWCA self-defense class. Finally I found it. I whipped it out, but it didn't stop my stalker. He took a step closer. I sprayed. Funny, it smelled just like mouthwash. Damn. It *was* mouthwash. I'd grabbed my Binaca by mistake!

"Calm down, Jaine. It's only me."

My would-be murderer stepped out of the shadows, and I saw that it wasn't Stan, but Detective Incorvia.

"Detective Incorvia," I said, flooded with relief. "What are you doing here?"

"Actually," he said, "I came to drop this off in your mailbox."

He held up a large manila envelope.

"It's my script," he said. "*Kung Fu Cop*. I was hoping you could read it and give me notes."

"I'm sorry, Detective Incorvia, but I make it a principle never to read scripts with the words 'Kung Fu' and 'Cop' in the same title."

Okay, so I didn't really say that. What I said was, "Sure. I'd be happy to."

"Did you get my message?" I asked.

"Yes, what's up?"

"I'm pretty sure Stan Miller is Quinn's killer. Last week, he was seen buying a box of rat poison."

"I know," he said. "We got a phone call from the owner of Beverly Hardware. Not only that, we found the box in the commissary dumpster. Stan's fingerprints were all over it."

"What about Audrey? Were her prints on the box, too?"

"No," he shook his head. "Nobody's prints were on the box. Nobody except Stan."

"And guess what?" I said. "I'm pretty sure he's the one who cut the wires on the klieg light."

"Really?"

"Yeah." And I told him about the "accident" on the set of *That Darn Hamlet*.

"Wow," Incorvia said when I was through. "It was the same kind of accident that happened to you the other night?"

"The exact same kind."

"And Stan was a lighting guy on the show?"

I nodded solemnly.

"It sure looks like Stan's our guy," he said.

It sure did, didn't it?

YOU'VE GOT MAIL!

TO: Jausten
FROM: Daddyo
SUBJECT: You're going to laugh when you hear this!

Sweetcakes, you're not going to believe this. The funniest thing just happened. I found that bottle of "love oil" in your mom's car. It was stuck way under the passenger seat. Anyhow, here's the funny part. It turns out it isn't love oil, after all. It's *Clove* Oil. It was an old bottle and the "C" on the label had worn off. It turns out your mom was using it after her trips to the dentist. Isn't that a hoot? Your mom's still a little miffed at me for "embarrassing" her on national TV. I guess I'm going to have to make it up to her somehow.

TO: Jausten
FROM: Shoptillyoudrop
SUBJECT: The Love Boat

Wonderful news, darling! Mr. Koskovalis has decided not to press charges! Which means Daddy is a free man!

And guess where Daddy is taking me? On a two-week cruise to the Carribean! He managed to get us last-minute tickets. Outer berths, with a verandah! So I guess you and I won't be roomies, after all. Not this time, anyway.

Send my best to Cookie, and give your darling kitty Zoloft a kiss for me.

Love, Mom

PS. Don't be mad, but I gave your phone number to Ernie Lindstrom.

Chapter
Twenty-Six

The cops arrested Stan on Friday, in the middle of a rewrite session. I'll never forget the look in his eyes as they read him his rights. Like a dog abandoned on the freeway. Puzzled, panicked, utterly bewildered. And in that moment, I knew—as sure as I knew that fudge was fattening—that Stan was innocent.

Yes, I know. Just last night I was convinced he was a cold-blooded killer, but if you'd seen him with that dazed look in his eyes, you'd know he couldn't possibly have killed anyone.

The cops led him out of the room—not handcuffed, thank goodness. Before he left, he took one last gulp from his Evian/gin bottle and stumbled over the threshold. See what I mean? The man had trouble walking from point A to point B; he simply couldn't have masterminded a murder.

The minute he was gone, Audrey reached for the phone and called her attorney. As always, her face was a mask. I couldn't tell whether she was overwhelmed with despair or glad to be rid of him. Kandi and I got up to go, to give her some privacy, but she gestured for us to stay. Quickly, efficiently, she told her attorney what had happened, and ordered him to line up the best defense team in town.

As I watched her on the phone, coolly dispensing instructions, I could easily picture Audrey as the killer. I remembered the "Q" I'd seen written in her appointment book on the date of the murder. It would be just like Audrey to allot a tidy time slot in her appointment book to remind herself she had a murder to commit:

> *Lunch at Spago.*
> *Network meeting.*
> *Kill Quinn.*
> *Bikini wax.*

So what if her fingerprints weren't on the box of poison? She could've wiped them off. Or worn gloves. Or used a whole other box of poison, for that matter.

Needless to say, I didn't contribute much to the rewrite session. Audrey was lucky I didn't haul her in on a citizen's arrest.

At last, we broke for lunch.

I heard Audrey tell Bianca that she was having lunch with her agent at the Bistro Gardens. I blinked in disbelief. Here her husband had just been arrested, and she was heading off with her agent to eat tuna nicoise!

The woman had ice in her veins.

Kandi and I headed to our office. Kandi was limp with relief. At last she was off the hook.

"Thank God it's all over," she said. "Now let's eat. Are you hungry? I'm starved!"

We went to lunch at the Four Seasons, Kandi's treat. They seated us out on the patio, a secluded oasis of lush greenery and exorbitant prices. Kandi ordered the cold poached salmon; I splurged on the coquilles St. Jacques. We washed down our lunch with chilled pinot grigio and polished it off with flourless chocolate cake, a dense fudgy concoction that lingers in my dreams to this day.

Thank goodness I'd worn a wrap skirt to work. By

the time they brought around the coffee, I'd loosened my waistband a good two inches.

As we lingered over our coffees in the dappled sunlight of the patio, I thought about my parents and that insane hoo-ha over a bottle of clove oil. By now, they were probably getting ready for their cruise, my mom packing enough cubic zirconia to blind her fellow passengers, and my father whipping up a twenty-minute pot roast to eat on the way to the ship.

The whole thing was so typical of my parents. They create a major life crisis, roiling with melodrama, and just when they've worried me half out of my wits, they say, "Haha, never mind, it was all a silly misunderstanding." In the words of my dear friend, H. Youngman: My parents don't have ulcers. They're just carriers.

And can you believe my mother—giving my phone number to Ernie Lindstrom? Now I'd have to spend the next few weeks dodging his calls.

Across the table, Kandi chattered on about how she'd never again take the good things in life for granted, how she fully intended to honor the deal she made with God to pursue noble causes, and how they were having a shoe sale at Bloomingdale's this weekend, and did I want to go?

I tried to be up and peppy, but my heart wasn't in it. Not after what happened this morning. I remembered the bewildered look in Stan's eyes as the cops led him away. I feared that the person responsible for Quinn's death was still on the loose, and felt helpless to do anything about it.

That afternoon, they had a memorial service for Quinn in the commissary. They'd taken out the tables and arranged the chairs into pewlike rows. It was like church, with a steam table. Kandi and I grabbed two seats near the exit, ready to escape in case things got too maudlin.

Everyone was there. The actors, the Beer Belly Brigade, the network guys, the cops from *PMS Squad*—even Helga, who sat picking wax from her ears with a bobby pin. Only Audrey was conspicuous by her absence.

"I heard there was an even bigger crowd at his burial," someone behind us said.

"Give the people what they want to see," Kandi muttered, "and they'll come out in droves."

Alan, the director, stood at a microphone that had been set up at the steam table. "We're all here," he said, "to say good-bye to a good friend and a fine actor. Quinn Kirkland was a consummate performer, a joy to work with."

As Alan went on to tell some highly fictional tales about what a great guy Quinn was, I looked around the room at my fellow mourners.

Dale sat, green around the gills, wearing sunglasses to hide what had to be a monumental hangover. Wells, on the other hand, had undergone a remarkable transformation. When I'd left him last night, he'd been a frail old man. Today, he was once more the urbane Brit, the kind of silver-haired senior citizen you see smiling from the pages of a retirement home brochure. Whatever vitamins he was taking, I wanted some.

Zach and Vanessa sat side by side, thighs touching, Zach's arm draped proprietarily over her shoulder. Vanessa's eyes were glazed with boredom; I was surprised she wasn't leafing through *Vogue*.

Vanessa's mother stood in the back of the room with the commissary staff, nervously fingering the buttons on her cardigan. And Bianca, normally such a cold bitch, was actually crying. Yes, big sloppy tears poured down her cheeks. I guess she really must have loved the guy. Either that, or she just broke a nail.

Alan finally wound down his eulogy and asked if there were any others who wanted to speak. An awkward silence filled the room. There were plenty of people who had something to say, I thought, but none of it repeatable in a churchlike setting.

Marco, the prop guy, got up and went to the mike. Marco was apparently one of those who'd been genuinely fond of Quinn.

"Not only was Quinn the best actor on the lot," he said, causing Dale to flinch behind his sunglasses, "Quinn was a terrific human being."

Kandi rolled her eyes.

"Mother Teresa in a jock strap," she muttered.

"When I think of how he gave of himself to other people . . ." Marco intoned.

"Right," Kandi whispered. "Sometimes as much as three times a night."

Bianca whirled around and glared at her.

"Will you please shut up?" she hissed.

Frankly, I was surprised at her outburst. It was the first time I'd ever heard her use the word "please."

"I guess what I'll remember most about Quinn," Marco said, "were his wonderful stories. Why, we used to sit here in the commissary and he'd have us all in stitches."

I thought back to my first day in the commissary, how excited I was to be having lunch at the same table with the handsome Quinn Kirkland. It seemed like centuries ago. I remembered how I sat listening to Dale and Wells and Quinn trading stories, vying in an unspoken competition to see who could get the biggest laughs.

Of course, Quinn—with his dazzling smile and perfect timing—had been the winner. He'd told about the chef in the restaurant who used to squeeze steaks under his armpit before he put them on the grill. And those practical jokes of his, when he worked as a valet parker in a Malibu restaurant, putting crazy things in the customers' glove compartments. Lace undies, smelly old chili dogs, and even a snake.

How funny those pranks seemed at the time. But now, looking back, they didn't seem funny at all. I mean, who the hell wants to find a rotting chili dog in her glove compartment? Or a snake? A person could get a heart attack from something like that.

And then it hit me. I knew who the real murderer was.

Just last night Wells told me his wife had suffered a fatal heart attack when she discovered a snake in her car. She'd been having lunch, he said, with friends in Malibu. What if it was the same Malibu restaurant where Quinn worked? What if, as a misguided prank, Quinn had put a snake in Jessica Dumont's glove compartment?

I could picture the scenario: On the way home, Jessica reaches for something in her glove compartment and sees the snake. Her heart gives out. All because of a stupid practical joke.

Wells's life is never the same. He goes through the motions, but his days are empty without the woman he loves. And then one day ten years later, he hears an arrogant actor bragging about how he put a snake in some poor shnook's glove compartment. He asks himself: Is it possible? Could it be? Could the snake in his wife's car have been left there by Quinn? Casually he chats with Quinn and asks him more about his job at the Malibu restaurant. He discovers that it's the same restaurant where his wife ate, and that Quinn had been working there at the time of her death. He knows that, however inadvertently, Quinn is responsible for his wife's death. And he vows to get revenge.

I looked over at Wells, watching Marco tell about the time Quinn filled a co-worker's bathtub with lime jello. For one brief instant I thought surely I must be mistaken. Wells was sitting back in his seat, an expansive smile on his face. The picture of good-natured ease.

But then I looked down and saw his hands, clenched so tightly I could see the white of his bones.

At that moment I knew with utter certainty that Wells had killed Quinn.

But what I couldn't figure out, not for the life of me, was how.

"You think Wells is the killer?"

Detective Incorvia's voice rose in disbelief, as if I'd just suggested that Queen Elizabeth was a pedophile.

As soon as the memorial service was over, I'd raced back to the Writers' Building and called him. And for once, he was actually at his desk.

"Wells couldn't have killed Quinn. His whereabouts were accounted for the entire time the prop room was left unattended. Several people saw him deep in conversation with Zach. When he wasn't talking to Zach, he was on stage doing his *Hamlet* soliloquy. And once taping started, he was on stage with Quinn in full view of the entire audience."

"Don't you think it's possible that he could have nipped in and out of the prop room for a minute or two, when no one was looking?"

"No, I don't think it's possible," Incorvia said. "The man is eighty years old, with bad feet. He doesn't nip in and out anywhere."

I had to admit he was right. I couldn't picture Wells making fast tracks anywhere—not without a motorized wheelchair.

My snake-in-the-glove-compartment theory was growing weaker by the minute.

"I appreciate all the help you've given us so far, Jaine. But this time, you're way off base. Wells Dumont had nothing whatsoever to do with Quinn's death."

"How can you be so sure?"

"Because Stan Miller just confessed."

"What?"

"He signed a full confession. Just twenty minutes ago."

I hung up, dumbfounded.

What the heck was Stan doing, confessing to a murder I knew he didn't commit? Had the police browbeat him? Had they promised him a martini, if only he'd sign on the dotted line?

Or was it possible that he really *was* the killer? Had I been totally wrong this morning? Did that look of utter bewilderment in Stan's eyes mean that he was simply an utterly bewildered killer? After all, there was no rule in the rulebooks that said you had to be a Rhodes Scholar to commit murder.

By now, I had absolutely no faith left in my powers of reasoning. Whatever made me think I was any good at this detective stuff anyway? Every other minute I was convinced someone new had committed the crime. First it was Dale. Then it was Vanessa and her mother. For five minutes, I was convinced it was Zach. And for a hopeful moment or two, Bianca had topped my list. Last night I could've sworn it was Stan. And just this morning I was prepared to personally put the handcuffs on Audrey. I'm surprised I didn't try to arrest Helga.

"Where the heck did you race off to?" Kandi said, coming in the office, eating a muffin. "You missed the free memorial buffet. I brought back a muffin for you."

She held out a blueberry muffin. I practically inhaled the damn thing.

"So," she said, "are you ready for your big night?"

"What big night?"

"The taping, dummy."

In all the excitement of the past few days, I'd forgotten: Tonight was the night they were taping my show.

Chapter Twenty-Seven

A fresh crop of tourists were sitting in the bleachers, waiting for "Cinderella Muffy" to begin. I thanked my lucky stars that Mr. Goldman wasn't one of them. The last thing I needed was an octogenarian heckler in the front row.

The warm-up guy was doing the same jokes he'd done last week. They hadn't gotten any funnier since then.

Kandi and I stood with Audrey near the cameras, scripts in hand. I scanned the audience, looking for hearty laughers, jolly souls chortling and poking each other, ready to giggle themselves silly. What I saw was a sea of American Gothic lookalikes—fair-haired, gimlet-eyed people who sat ramrod straight, eerily silent.

"Oh, dear," I said to Kandi. "Who are these people, and why aren't they smiling?"

"They're Mormons," Kandi said.

"Mormons?"

"Yeah, they're here on a break from Bible Study Camp."

"Oh, great," I wailed. "There go my laughs."

"Don't worry," Kandi said. "That's what laugh tracks are for. We'll just sweeten the show later."

I was standing there, wishing they'd shoot me instead of the show, when I heard someone call out:

"Yoo-hoo, Jaine!"

I looked up. There in the front row, smack dab in the middle of the Mormons, was Lance Venable.

"C'mere!" he hissed, motioning me to come over. I smiled feebly and headed in his direction. Damn. What if he found out I didn't give his treatment to Audrey in person, that I'd slipped it onto her desk like a thief in the night? But I was being ridiculous; there was no way he could possibly find out.

"Hi, Lance!" I said, trying to look as if I were happy to see him. "What are you doing here?"

"I didn't want to miss your show biz debut. Say hi to my friend Peter."

His friend Peter was a stunning black man with a diamond stud in his ear. He and Lance stood out from the Mormons like two croissants in a Wonder Bread factory.

"Omigosh," Lance said, "is that your boss? The blonde in the white suit?"

I nodded.

"I know her!"

Damn.

"You do?"

"She's one of my customers."

"Yoo-hoo, Audrey!" he shouted, waving at her.

Audrey glanced up from where she was consulting with the director. I told myself not to panic. Never in a million years would she come over and say hello. Audrey never mingled with the common people.

Then why the hell was she walking over in our direction with a big smile plastered on her face?

"Lance, sweetie," she said. "It's so nice to see you."

"When Jaine told me her boss was named Audrey, I had no idea it was you!" Lance said. "Did you get a chance to read my treatment?"

"What treatment?"

"Didn't Jaine give it to you?"

"No, she sure didn't."

Lance looked at me, daggers in his eyes.

"Uh . . . I left it on your desk," I stammered. "*If the Shoe Fits*. About a bunch of shoe salesmen."

"I wondered where that came from." Audrey beamed at Lance. "It's hilarious!"

What? Had the world gone mad, or just Audrey? *If the Shoe Fits* was about as funny as a barium enema. Maybe she was just being nice to him so he'd give her a good deal on some Ferragamos.

"I think we can sell it to Fox." Good heavens, it sounded like she meant it. "I'll call you and we'll do lunch."

Then she blew him a kiss and headed back to the director.

I didn't know what to be more flabbergasted over: the fact that she actually liked Lance's shoe saga, or the fact that she didn't seem to give a damn that her husband was festering in jail, a confessed murderer.

But I didn't have time to stay flabbergasted for long, because just then, the warm-up guy announced that the taping of "Cinderella Muffy" was about to begin.

I'm happy to report that Act One zipped by without a single dead body cropping up on stage.

What's more, the Mormons were wonderful! Yes, those delightful people laughed at all my jokes—and some of the straight lines, too. I guess after being holed up in Bible Camp, they were ready to laugh at anything. Or maybe they were simply discerning connoisseurs of comedy. All I know is that they were a fabulous audience, and the next time they show up on my doorstep wanting to discuss the Bible, I'm going to ask them in for coffee and danish.

My spirits were lifting. Judging from the response of my darling Mormons, it looked like I had a lucrative career as a sitcom writer ahead of me.

The warm-up guy was back on stage, doing some magic tricks, waiting for the crew to set up for Act Two. Unlike his jokes, his magic tricks were pretty good. I watched as he took a quarter from a church elder's hairy ear. It really did look like the coin was coming out from the guy's ear. Magicians are amazing, I thought, in their ability to fool the eye.

And then I remembered:

Wells had been a magician.

Just last night, in his scrapbook, I'd seen a picture of him as "Dumont the Great."

And suddenly I knew how Wells had killed Quinn.

Everyone assumed the donut had been poisoned in the prop room. But what if the fatal dose of poison had been sprinkled *on stage*, with a magician's sleight of hand, in full view of the entire audience?

When Quinn had offered Wells the box of donuts, the audience saw him waving it away. What they didn't see was Wells sprinkling rat poison into the box. And with the raised lid of the box facing Quinn, he wouldn't have noticed either. That, I was certain, was how Wells had killed Quinn Kirkland.

The rest of the taping went by in a blur. I simply couldn't concentrate on the script. All I could think about was Wells. I told myself I was being foolish. After all, Stan had confessed to the crime. Wells was a lonely old man with good hair and bad feet; why couldn't I leave the poor guy alone? He was simply the latest in a long line of my Suspects du Jour. I really had to forget about Quinn's death. I had a whole new career ahead of me, and I couldn't afford to blow it over some cocka-mamie murder theory.

Before I knew it, the taping was over. The Mormons were filing out of the soundstage, still chuckling at Muffy's zany adventures.

That's where my future was, I told myself—in laughs,

not deaths. After such a positive audience response, Audrey was sure to offer me a staff job.

Which is why I was optimistic when Audrey called the cast and crew together.

"People," she said, "I've got an announcement to make."

Could it be? Was she going to thank me for a wonderful script and offer me a staff job right here in front of everybody?

"The show's been cancelled," she said.

Apparently not.

Gasps of disappointment and surprise filled the air.

"The network just called. Too much negative publicity. First the murder, and then the incident with the overhead light." She eyed me balefully, as if blaming me for almost getting my head bashed in.

"Well, that's it," she said, showing about as much emotion as a paperweight. "Better pack up and clear out tonight. The party's over."

So much for my budding sitcom career.

But here's the crazy part: I didn't care. So what if I wasn't exactly Sherlock Holmes? I *liked* being a detective. If truth be told, I liked it a lot more than I liked writing sitcoms. And right now, I had a case to solve. I was convinced that Wells was Quinn's killer.

Now all I had to do was get him to confess.

Chapter
Twenty-Eight

"**D**amnphooeyfuckshit! Now I'll have to go back to writing for the cockroach."

We were back in our office and Kandi was stretched out on the sofa, staring morosely into space, bemoaning her fate. What with *Muffy 'n Me* cancelled, she'd be forced to go back to her old job writing for *Beanie & The Cockroach*.

"Do you know what it's like spending your days writing cockroach jokes?" She sighed with great drama.

"Hey," I said. "Do you know how many people slinging fries at McDonald's would kill for a job as an animation writer? What happened to your vow to never again sweat the small stuff if only God would get you off the hook for murder?"

She had the grace to look somewhat abashed.

"You're right," she said, sitting up. "I'm being very spoiled-brattish. Just yesterday I thought I'd be spending the rest of my life in jail fighting off advances from women with mustaches. What's wrong with me, anyway? I have absolutely no sense of perspective. So what if I have to write jokes for a household pest? So what if the only people who see my name on the credits have Cream of Wheat dribbling onto their bibs? So what if I have to go groveling back to my old boss, the one who told me, *You'll come groveling back to me, just wait and see.*

"Oh, hell," she said, suddenly back in the valley of depression. "I need a drink."

"Congratulations. You managed to keep things in perspective for a whole four and a half seconds."

"What can I say?" she shrugged. "I'm hopeless."

She went to her desk and fished a bottle of tequila from the bottom drawer.

"Cocktail time," she said, holding it aloft.

We managed to find some orange juice in the office refrigerator and made ourselves makeshift Tequila Sunrises, a normally festive drink that seems a lot less festive when you're drinking it out of a *Muffy 'n Me* coffee mug.

Back in our office, we spent several companionable moments sipping our Tequila Sunrises and watching the transvestites strut their stuff on Santa Monica Boulevard.

A muscular man in stiletto heels, fishnet stockings, and a Tina Turner wig was leaning into the open window of a Mercedes to negotiate a price for his services. His black leather skirt was cut so tight, you could practically read the label on his jockstrap.

Starting next week, the guy would be making more money than me.

"Well," Kandi said, draining the last of her Tequila Sunrise, "I guess it's time to get packing."

We tossed most of her *Muffy 'n Me* scripts in the trash.

"No need to save them for posterity," she sighed.

Then we wrapped her personal belongings in our chair towels and carried them out to her car, hobo style. There wasn't much to carry. When we were through loading her trunk, I took what would surely be my last look around the Miracle lot.

"Good-bye, hookers!" I said, saluting the gang on Santa Monica Boulevard. "Good-bye rubber sandwiches at the commissary. Good-bye, Haunted House. Good-bye, roller coaster—"

And as I turned to salute the roller coaster, I saw someone standing at the ride's control box. A man with silvery hair that glinted in the moonlight.

"Hey. Isn't that Wells?"

"Yeah," Kandi said. "I think it is."

"Wait a minute. I'll be right back."

I hurried over to the roller coaster. Sure enough, it was Wells. He was bent over the control box, trying to pry it open with a crowbar.

"Wells! What's going on?"

He looked up and smiled calmly, as if he always went around prying roller coaster controls open with a crowbar.

"Jaine, my dear. What a lovely surprise."

"What are you doing?"

"Taking a roller coaster ride."

His eyes sparkled with a slightly maniacal glint.

"Look, Wells," I said. "This is really awkward, and I don't know how to put it, but I was wondering . . ."

"Yes?"

"Did you . . . uh . . . happen to kill Quinn?"

Good heavens. I really had to work on my detective patter.

"As a matter of fact, my dear, I did."

He grunted with the effort of maneuvering the crowbar. The control box was big, and the metal door was heavy.

"After all," he said, "Quinn was responsible for Jessica's death. I couldn't let him get away with murder, could I?"

His brow glistened with sweat as he worked the crowbar back and forth. Somehow he'd tapped into a hidden reserve of strength. It was like one of those stories where a ninety-eight-pound mother lifts a truck to save her baby.

"It was really quite easy. I hid the vial of poison up my sleeve. No one ever suspected. Dumont the Great performing his finest feat of magic."

He gave one final heave to the crowbar, and the metal door sprang open.

"Aha!" He grinned like a kid breaking into his piggy bank.

"And the klieg light," I said. "Are you the one who tried to drop it on me?"

He blinked in surprise.

"Of course not, my dear. I'd never dream of hurting you. I have no idea who was responsible for that dastardly deed."

And I believed him.

"And now," he said, "if you'll excuse me, it's time to say *adieu*. Not *au revoir*, but *adieu*. I trust you know the difference."

He trusted wrong. I had no idea what the heck he was trying to say. I don't exactly run around with a French–English dictionary in my purse. But if I did, I would have known that *au revoir* means *till next we meet*, and *adieu* means *Farewell Forever, Ta-ta Tootsie, The End, Fini, Don't Bother to Write*. Or words to that effect.

He pulled a lever and the ancient motor groaned to life.

"What are you doing?" I called out as he headed for the roller coaster.

"I'm going to kill myself, of course."

"What?"

"I can't let Stan go to jail for a murder he didn't commit. I've got a suicide note right here," he said, patting his shirt pocket. "A short but succinct document wherein I confess my sins."

He looked up to the top of the roller coaster, which suddenly seemed awfully high to me.

"And in case my note gets . . . uh . . . messy, I left a

copy on my bureau. Right next to my blood pressure medication. Make sure the police see it, will you, my dear?"

And with that he leaped into one of the carts.

Oh, God. He was going to jump. I'd once read a story in the paper about a teenager who'd tried to jump to his death from a ride at Disneyland. And now Wells was about to do the same thing.

The roller coaster began its slow ascent up the first steep hill.

And then I did something incredibly stupid. Something I surely wouldn't have done if I hadn't just polished off a Tequila Sunrise. The roller coaster had begun moving, but the last cart was still on level ground. Call me crazy, but I climbed on board. I just couldn't let the poor old guy kill himself.

Wells was up front in the first cart, reciting what I could only assume was Shakespeare:

> *I have liv'd long enough. My way of life*
> *Is fallen into the sere, the yellow leaf;*
> *And that which should accompany old age,*
> *As honor, love, obedience, troops of friends,*
> *I must not look to have.*

"Don't jump, Wells!" I shouted.

But he didn't hear me over the din of the grinding cables.

Somehow I'd have to manage to get into Wells's cart. Forcing myself not to look down, I climbed out from my cart and into the one in front of me. Which wasn't easy with that damn wrap skirt of mine flapping in the breeze. I repeated this utterly terrifying process until I was at last in the cart behind him.

"Don't do it, Wells!"

He turned around and saw me for the first time.

"Get off!" he shouted angrily. "Get off!"

"You mustn't kill yourself, Wells. With a good attorney and a sympathetic jury, you could be free in a few years."

He laughed bitterly.

"Free? Free to do what? Free to come home to an empty house night after night? Free to play small parts in pathetic sitcoms? Free to spend the rest of my life watching my body fall apart? No, my dear. It's time for me to go. I've been planning this for a long time. No clichéd death with sleeping pills for me. I'm going to go out fighting, like my beloved Macbeth."

"No!" I shouted, as I climbed into his cart and held down the safety bar. "I can't let you jump."

His eyes widened in surprise.

"Jump?" he said. "Who said anything about jumping? I cut one of the cables."

"What?"

"As soon as we reach the top of the hill, we're going to crash to our deaths."

Oh, damn! NOW he tells me!

By now we were just a few feet away from the crest. I scrambled desperately to get out of the cart and grab hold of the wooden siding. But I couldn't reach it.

"You'll have to stand on the edge of the cart," Wells said. "Don't worry. I'll hold you."

And he did. In a final act of chivalry, he kept my legs braced while I reached out for the elusive wooden siding. Finally I was able to grab hold of it. Then he let go of my legs, and I managed to get a toehold to safety.

Wells Dumont may have killed Quinn Kirkland, but that night he saved my life.

"*Adieu,* my dear," he said blowing me a kiss. "Don't be sad. This is the way I want it."

Then he sat back down in the cart, his spine straight, his eyes bright with anticipation, as if riding a horse to battle.

The roller coaster reached the crest.

"Lay on, Macduff!" he shouted, brandishing an invisible sword. "And damn'd be him that first cries 'Hold, enough!' "

And then, before my eyes, Wells Dumont plummeted to his death.

Chapter
Twenty-Nine

A word to the wise: Never hang from the side of a roller coaster in a denim wrap skirt.

By now a crowd had gathered down below, all of them looking straight up into the all-cotton crotch of my control-top pantyhose. Gad, how mortifying.

Kandi had called 911, and before long a rather attractive Marlboro Mannish fireman was climbing a ladder, telling me to stay calm.

Easy for him to say. He wasn't clinging for dear life to a pile of termite-infested popsicle sticks.

Finally, he made it to the top of the ladder and managed to extricate me from my precarious perch. Step by step he guided me down the ladder, all the while treated to the aforementioned view of my crotch.

At last I was on terra firma, just in time to see the cops swarming around Wells's body.

"I'm sorry I didn't believe you, Jaine." I turned to see Detective Incorvia, looking rather sheepish. "We found a suicide note in his pocket. He confessed to everything."

"That's okay," I said. "I had a hard time believing it myself. Wells was such a nice guy."

"I hope you realize he had nothing to do with cutting the wire on the klieg light."

"I know," I said.

"Stan did that. I just got off the phone with him. I told him about Wells, and he recanted his confession. Except for the part about the klieg light. He swears, though, that he never meant to hit you. All he wanted was to get *Muffy 'n Me* cancelled. He thought if he could get Audrey to retire to Palm Springs, he could save their marriage."

"But I don't understand why he confessed to Quinn's murder."

"Apparently, he thought Audrey was the killer. He'd bought the rat poison—innocently enough—to kill rats. Then, after Quinn was murdered, he thought Audrey had used the stuff to knock off Quinn. He'd overheard her threatening to get rid of him, and he was afraid she'd lived up to her threat. Which is why he foolishly threw the box of poison into the dumpster with his prints all over it."

"So he confessed to protect her."

"The things we do for love, huh?"

"Yeah," I sighed, reminding myself to pick up some crabmeat for Prozac on my way home. "The things we do for love."

"Well, it's been nice working with you, Jaine."

We shook hands good-bye, and then he walked back to where poor Wells's body was being loaded in to the coroner's truck.

"Excuse me, miss."

It was the Marlboro Man fireman, holding a clipboard. "If you don't mind, I'm going to need a few facts for my report."

I couldn't help noticing his eyes, which were a beautiful hazel with flecks of brown, like chocolate jimmies on pistachio ice cream.

"Your name?"

"Jaine. Jaine Austen."

"No kidding!" His eyes widened with surprise.

"I know, I know. You love my books."

"Actually," he said, "I was just going to call you."

"You were?"

"Yeah. Your mom gave me your phone number. Didn't she tell you?"

My eyes shot to his name tag.

"I'm Ernie," he grinned. "Ernie Lindstrom."

Epilogue

Thanks to the machinations of his high-powered attorney, Stan wound up serving less than a year in jail. During which time he lost twenty pounds and gave up booze. By the time he got out of jail, Audrey had started divorce proceedings, but Stan didn't mind. Three months after his release, he married his parole officer.

Audrey went on to produce a string of forgettable sitcoms. Lance's wasn't one of them. In fact, after the night of the taping, he never heard from her again.

After *Muffy* folded, Vanessa played the corpse in a teen slasher movie, and Zach Levy-Taylor got himself a gig on a long-running soap opera. He plays a guy named Brick, a moniker which I think suits his acting talents to a T.

Dale was unemployed for a while, but finally landed himself a gig doing infomercials for the Turbo Steamer. He's now my father's favorite TV star.

Kandi is back writing for the cockroach and, incidentally, dating a guy she met in Dr. Mellman's waiting room.

And Bianca is still picking up Audrey's dry cleaning.

As for me, I've resumed my old life, writing resumes and brochures. Perhaps you've read my latest:

Only YOU Can Prevent Clogged Toilets! I still teach my memoir-writing class at the Shalom Retirement Home. Mr. Goldman is as insufferable as ever, bragging that he knew all along "whodunit." And, as galling as it is to admit, he did. He'd always said the murderer was Wells.

I dated Ernie Lindstrom for a while. After a few months he decided he wanted to get married. Unfortunately, not to me, but to a nymphette he met while putting out a fire at a Swedish massage parlor.

Sometimes, at the end of the day, when I'm sitting in my living room sipping a chardonnay and enjoying the view of my neighbor's azalea bush, I think about what my life would have been like as a high-paid sitcom writer, with a fancy car and a Malibu beach house and a closetful of Joan & David shoes. But then I remember what life was like at Miracle Studios—the monumental egos, the petty jealousies, and those godawful rubber sandwiches. And I realize that there's no way I'd ever go back to all that Hollywood crap.

Unless, of course, somebody offered me a job.

PS. I almost forgot. Detective Incorvia sold *Kung Fu Cop* to Dreamworks for $3.5 million.

Please turn the page for an exciting sneak peek of

Laura Levine's next Jaine Austen mystery

KILLER BLONDE

coming next month in hardover!

Prologue

My name is Jaine, and I'm a bathaholic.

Yes, it's true. I like nothing better than to tear off my clothes in the middle of the afternoon and leap into a hot bubble bath. So it's lucky I'm a freelance writer. While other working stiffs are trapped in offices, chained to their computers, I can hop into the tub any time I please.

Which is what I was doing the day SueEllen Kingsley first called me. I'd just finished writing a slogan for a new client, Tip Top Dry Cleaners *(We'll clean for you. We'll press for you. We'll even dye for you.)*, and I was relaxing in a marvelous haze of strawberry-scented bubbles. The mirrors were fogged over. The radio, if I remember correctly, was playing a soulful Diana Krall love song. And my cat Prozac was perched on top of the toilet tank, licking her privates, visions of fish guts dancing in her head.

It was one of those blissful moments I often experience after I've finished a writing assignment, basking in the glow of a job well done (or done, anyway), until it dawns on me that now that the assignment is over, I'm out of work again.

I was still in the bask-in-the-glow stage when the phone rang. I let the machine get it.

"Ms. Austen." A syrupy, southern-accented voice drifted out from the machine. "SueEllen Kingsley here. I saw your ad in the yellow pages—"

Yippee! A prospective client!

"And I'm calling because I need a ghostwriter to help me write a book."

At the sound of the word "ghostwriter," my enthusiasm came to a screeching halt. In my experience, people who are looking for ghostwriters often fall into the "mentally unstable" category. These are people who want to tell the world about how they were abducted to the planet Clorox and forced to have sex with spatulas. Or people who believe that they're the love child of Wayne Newton and Golda Meir.

SueEllen Kingsley left her number on my machine. For a minute I considered not returning the call. But then I remembered a few pesky facts of life, like my rent and my Visa bill and my impossible-to-kick Ben & Jerry's Chunky Monkey habit.

Reluctantly, I hauled myself out of the tub and into a worn chenille bathrobe. Then I shuffled over to the phone and dialed.

If I'd known what I was getting into, I would've stayed up to my eyeballs in soapsuds.

Chapter One

SueEllen Kingsley answered the phone, her voice as gooey as melted Velveeta. "Ms. Austen," she oozed, "can you hustle your fanny over to my house in an hour?"

I assured her I was an expert at fanny-hustling, and she gave me the directions to her house. Which turned out to be more like a castle. A vintage Spanish estate nestled in one of Beverly's niftiest Hills, the house was a showstopper. Its arches and balustrades and red tile roof glistened in the midafternoon sun. The whole thing was so Spanish manor-ish, I almost expected to see Zorro leap onto one of the many balconies with a rose in his teeth. But there was no sign of Zorro. The only Hispanic in sight was a gardener pruning the bougainvillea.

I drove up a circular driveway and parked my humble Corolla next to a gleaming Bentley. Then I checked my teeth in my rear view mirror for any stray pieces of lettuce left over from the Jumbo Jack I'd picked up on my way over. Satisfied that all was clear on the dental front, I gave myself a quick blast of Binaca and tugged a few unruly curls back into my ponytail.

Finally, plucking a stray french fry from my lap, I got out of the Corolla and looked around. What a palace. The kind of place God would build if He had money.

I was beginning to regret my decision to wear my

usual work outfit of jeans and a blazer. A place like this called for something a lot fancier. Like the British crown jewels and a blazer.

Why the heck was a woman with SueEllen's money calling a writer from the Yellow Pages? I'd checked her out on Google before I left my apartment, and found her name scattered on the society pages of the *Los Angeles Times*. SueEllen was apparently a partygiver and fund-raiser par excellence. Surely she had access to scads of well-known writers. So why, I asked myself again, had she called anonymous old me? Oh, well. Who cared why she called? Just as long as her check didn't bounce. And from the looks of the place, I was sure it wouldn't.

I headed up the front path, and rang the bell.

Now I don't know if they have a doorbell at Versailles, but if they do, I'll bet it sounds just like the Kingsleys'. A series of mellifluous bongs resonated from inside the house. Seconds later the door was opened by a timid Hispanic maid holding a bottle of Windex.

"Hi," I smiled. "I'm Jaine Austen. I have an appointment with Mrs. Kingsley."

"Si," she said, eyes lowered, clutching her Windex to her chest. She spoke softly, in a heavily accented voice. "Mrs. Kinglsey's having her massage. She wants you to wait in the living room."

I followed her as we hiked across the foyer. A wide curving staircase with gleaming mahogany banisters ascended to the floor above. I almost expected to see Scarlett O'Hara come skipping down the steps, twirling her parasol.

The living room was huge, with hardwood floors, an exposed wood beam ceiling, and a fireplace as big as my kitchen. I took a seat in one of the many overstuffed armchairs dotted throughout the room. The maid asked me if I wanted anything to drink, and seemed relieved when I said no.

As she skittered away, presumably to do battle with dirty windows, I glanced down and saw a grease stain on my blouse. Probably from the french fry that dropped in my lap. Oh, great. Now I'd have to spend the entire interview with my blazer buttoned. Which wasn't going to be easy, since I'd bought the blazer two sizes too small. It was on sale at Ann Taylor, the only one they had left, reduced seventy percent. I went ahead and bought it, figuring I'd never have to button the damn thing.

Now I sucked in my gut, and was struggling with the buttons when I heard:

"You'll never last a week."

I looked across the room and for the first time I noticed a young girl nestled in an armchair underneath a huge bay window.

She was a chubby kid, about 15, with soft brown eyes and an old fashioned Dutch Boy haircut. Something about her looked vaguely familiar. And then I realized—Good heavens, she was me—at fifteen. Not that I have brown eyes; mine are green. And when I was 15, I wasn't quite as chunky as this girl. But there was something about her that reminded me of the young Jaine Austen. Maybe it was the book she was reading. *Stiff Upper Lip,* by the British humorist P.G. Wodehouse. When I was a teenager, I was crazy about his books. In fact, I still am. But it's not every day you see a teenager reading Wodehouse.

"Nobody ever lasts a week," she said, looking up at me from under her thick bangs. "Sooner or later, they all quit."

So that's why SueEllen was willing to hire a writer from the Yellow Pages. No reputable writer would work for her.

"She's nice at first, but then she turns mean. You'll see."

"So your mom's tough to work for, huh?"

The kid looked at me as if I'd just offered her a worm for lunch.

"SueEllen isn't my mother," she said with all the warmth of Christina Crawford talking about Joan. "She's my stepmother. My real mother's dead."

"I'm sorry."

"Yeah," she said. "Me, too."

And with that she picked up her book and began reading. Conversation terminated.

"Miss Austen?"

The Hispanic maid was at the door, still clutching her Windex. I only wished she had some stain remover for the grease spot on my blouse.

"Mrs. Kingsley will see you now," she said.

I got up to go. I tried to button my blazer, but it was no use. SueEllen Kingsley would have to accept me as I was, grease stain and all.

"Nice meeting you," I said to the kid in the chair.

"Whatever," was her jolly reply.

I followed the maid up a flight of stairs and down what seemed like an endless hallway. If I'd known how big this place was, I would've worn hiking shoes.

Halfway down the corridor, we ran into a bubbly blonde carrying a portable massage table. She weighed about as much as my right leg.

"Hi, Conchi," she said to the maid. Then she turned to me, beaming me an impossibly white smile. "I'm Larkspur O'Leary, SueEllen's masseuse."

Larkspur O'Leary? And I thought my mom was bad naming me Jaine Austen.

"You must be the new writer," she said.

"No, not exactly. I'm just here for an interview. I haven't got the job yet."

"Oh, you will. You look very capable. And besides, SueEllen's desperate."

She beamed me another smile, almost blinding me in the process.

"Here's my card." She handed me a pastel pink business card, with her name printed in a flowery script. "I use a special method of massage that breaks down the fat cells and gets rid of cellulite." She let her glance linger on my thighs, which, I have to admit, are home to a happy colony of fat cells.

"Thanks. I'll keep that in mind."

"Well, see ya," she said. Then she started down the hallway, swinging her massage table as if it were a bag of Fritos. For a tiny thing, she was awfully strong.

"Oh, and good luck," she called back. And then she added, with a wink, "You're going to need it."

I smiled weakly and followed Conchi down the endless hallway. At last we reached our destination. Conchi opened the door to a bathroom straight out of *Architectural Digest*, gleaming with marble, gold fixtures and light streaming in from overhead skylights. At first I thought she'd taken leave of her senses. Why on earth would she be bringing me to the bathroom? Clearly the woman had been sniffing too many Windex fumes.

"Ms. Austen, I presume?"

I looked over and saw my prospective employer, Sue-Ellen Kingsley, stretched out in a tub so big, it could hold the entire cast of *Friends*, and still have room left over for Drew Carey.

The first thing I noticed about SueEllen were her boobs. Two perfect pink globes, bobbing in the water like cantaloupes. Later I would notice her tawny hair, her tiny waist, and her fine-boned face with an unlikely smattering of freckles on her nose. But not at first. No, all I saw at first were those incredible boobs.

"Like 'em?" Sue Ellen asked, following my gaze. "They're a birthday gift from my husband."

Talk about a gift for the gal who has everything.

"Hal's a plastic surgeon. All the stars go to him. He gives great liposuction," she added, taking a none too discreet glance at my thighs.

I was getting a bit miffed at the way everybody seemed to be taking potshots at my thighs. Okay, so I'm no supermodel, but that doesn't mean I don't have feelings.

"That'll be all, Conchi," SueEllen said, waving the maid away with her loofah sponge.

Conchi scurried out of the room, like an infantryman trying to stay out of the line of fire.

"Have a seat," SueEllen said, gesturing to the toilet bowl. I sat down on the toilet lid, crossing my arms over my chest to hide the grease spot on my blouse, and trying not to look as uncomfortable as I felt.

"I hope you don't mind my interviewing you in the bathroom," SueEllen said.

"Not at all," I lied.

"But this is where I work," she said, washing between her toes. "I get my best ideas in the bathtub."

"Me, too, actually. It's where I thought up the slogan for one of my biggest clients, Toiletmasters Plumbers."

Okay, so Toiletmasters wasn't exactly a Fortune 500 company. But at the moment, it was the shining star on my resume.

"*In a rush to flush? Call Toiletmasters!* You thought of that?"

I nodded modestly; the woman was actually impressed.

"That's wonderful, honey. I can see you're just oozing with talent. Have you ever ghostwritten a book?"

"Yes," I said. "Once."

"What was it about?"

"Uh, it was sort of a . . . memoir."

Please don't let her ask me what it was called.

"What was it called?"

I took a deep breath, and spat it out. (Sensitive readers may want to skip the following sentence.)

"*I Was Henry Kissinger's Sex Slave.*"

"Really?" SueEllen said. "So was I!"

"What?"

"Only kidding," she said, laughing at her own gag, her incredible breasts bouncing like buoys in the ocean.

"Ha ha," I managed weakly.

"I suppose you want to know what my book is about."

"Of course."

"It's about entertaining."

I smiled a genuine smile of relief, grateful that there were no space aliens involved.

"Sounds great."

"Oh, it will be," she said, sudsing a long lean cellulite-free thigh. "You are looking at the next Martha Stewart. I don't know if you've ever seen my name in the papers, but I'm just about the most popular hostess on the Beverly Hills party circuit. People kill for invitations to my parties. So now I'm going to share my entertaining secrets with the public. I'll give recipes and talk about how to hire a caterer and tell all sorts of marvelous anecdotes from my past. I've led a very colorful life, you know."

I didn't doubt that for a minute.

"So how about it," she said. "You interested?"

"What exactly did you have in mind as a salary?"

"Three thousand."

"I don't know," I said. "Three thousand dollars isn't much. After all, the book will take months to write."

"Not three thousand for the whole book, silly. Three thousand a week."

Suddenly, the toilet didn't seem so uncomfortable after all.

Grab These
Kensington Mysteries